Sensuous Voyager

Sensuous Voyager

by

Roberta Williams

Copyright © 1982 by Siena Publishing Corp.

TIGRESS BOOKS are published by
Siena Publishing Corp.
New York, New York

ISBN: 0-503-02017-6

Printed in the United States of America

Covers posed for by professional models

CHAPTER ONE

Ever been to your father's wedding?

It's a true rush to see the old man all dressed up in morning coat and striped trousers, fidgeting around like a kid. And watching the bride's brother from Passaic walk her up the aisle. (No, as a matter of fact she wore a pale-blue dress. Last week I had suggested off-white trimmed in red—and I just managed to duck her fistic comment.)

And there was her daughter, Janey, developed quite nicely at eighteen, thank you. She was a super specimen of pulchritude, and when I noted her batting her eyes at me, I was happy she was of legal age, just in case. Oh boy. And a lot of relatives, and friends, and an assortment of people from Dad's business, along with others who were there strictly for business reasons and because Dad is, after all, Loren P. Holliman.

The best man, believe it or not, wasn't shook. A little tired, maybe, but not uptight or shook. The best man did not lose the ring. I stuck my hand in my pocket and there it was, right where I'd put it. I passed it over to Dad, and then my eyebrows started climbing my forehead. I've wondered ever since who else noticed that Dad didn't slipped that ring on Mindy's finger.

She *rammed* her finger right through that classy hole.

I had to bite back my grunt. Even the minister twitched. Something like a half tingle jumped up through my crotch. *Forget it, Lance-baby,* I told myself. *That ball-tingler just became your step-mommy!*

They did their obligatory face-sucking, my old man and his bride, both of them two-time losers, and then she turned to me. I think I surprised her by giving her a chaste and sweet little kiss.

"I wuv you mommy," I murmured, and got a look that made me fear spontaneous combustion.

But that was it, without a hitch. That was that with Mindy Simpson. Now she was Mindy Holliman, and not Mrs. *Lancelot P.,* either.

We wended our ceremonious way out of the church, and all the way over to the reception I was quiet, pensive. Thinking about Dad. And me. And Mindy. And last night.

I had pretended to drink a lot more than I really did at Dad's bachelor party. The grass I sneaked in the little kitchen of Mark's bachelor digs helped. It

6

loosens me up, makes me talkative and sort of limp-legged, as if I'm drunk—but it wears off quickly.

Naturally none of those laughing, yokking, dirty-joking guys had wanted to take me home, which was just what I'd counted on. They got me a cab and gave the grinning driver the address and went back to kid Dad about who was really the best man. The address they laid on the driver was the Hilton, the big museumlike monstrosity they perpetrated for the world's fair. Dad and I had a suite on the fifth floor.

Mindy was staying up in six-oh-seven.

The driver was surprised when his passenger seemed to sober up during that short ride through town. I crossed his palm with too much green, went into the hotel, played drunky while I collected one of the keys to our suite, and boarded one of the elevators the N.Y. Hilton people keep hidden in a short blind corridor.

I punched Six and clung to my gut as the elevator did its thing. Then I was walking straight down the corridor to Mindy's room.

Her daughter, Janey, was staying with an aunt, some ten blocks away at the Algonquin. Aunt Dot thought maybe she would see an Authah down there in that old dump with the swollen room-rates. What she'd see, mostly, was a lot of worn carpets and ancient furniture! And that nice, white-haired Japanese elevator "boy."

Mindy answered my knock at once. I was delighted to learn that she had departed her own bachelor party so early.

7

Mindy was sort of wearing a floor-length white film of a negligee that must have contained ten yards of gauzy nylon. She hadn't belted it; it hung beautifully and sexily loose. She was also tucked into that white half-bra with the covering of transparent black net, decorated with opaque black roses.

(Yes, I do remember it well. It had wide-set black straps that left her bare all across the uplands of her chest and cuddled something like two-thirds of the soft flesh of her tits together, raised high and jiggly. You remember that kind of bra. It does more for a woman's frontispiece than Mama Nature ever did for most, and speaks eloquently against the bra-less look.)

Her more essential parts were clutched in fire-engine red panties that were so tight and skimpy they looked like they belonged to her eighteen-year old daughter—last year.

"Jesus," I said after our tonguey kiss, "get those incredible panties off. They look like something you took off a whore down on Avenue B."

She laughed, twirling so that the cloud of peignoir stood out from her in spiderweb billows. Mindy was vain about her showgirl legs. Still is. She has a right.

"Are there actually whores on Avenue B?"

"Sure there are. They just don't charge," I advised her, doing things about getting out of my jacket then dragging my shirttails out of my pants.

"Oh, well then," she said, stopping her pirouette to sizzle me a low-lidded look from those sexy eyes of hers. "Neither do I."

8

"The hell you don't." I slung my shirt over an expensive chair. Everything's expensive in the New York Hilton. It's one of those so-swanky places in which the help puts on a sneer every morning, along with clothing. "You're charging Dad a white-gold ring!"

"It's platinum," Mindy corrected me, "with twelve diamonds. Tastefully small ones. I had a plain gold band, my first marriage. There. Is that better?"

I smiled. It was infinitely better. She'd gotten out of those godawful scarlet briefs. She had a bedazzling, even intimidating muff, Mindy did. A conspicuous mound well-fledged with a full bush that covered the bulge, which was an emphatic pink. The crack of her sex was visible only as a faint center parting of that rich brown bush, like the little furrow in the center of my mustache. Her labia weren't visible at all, although I well knew that those hungry lips were there, ready to grab onto a cockhead and inhale it up her prehensile vagina.

I hoped sincerely that Dad would be careful to keep that throbbing fissure well plugged up with his fructifier. Otherwise he was going to have trouble on his hands; Mindy was a hot woman.

I had been keeping her ever-smoldering furnace well stoked for the past six months, on a very regular basis. As a matter of fact that's how Dad met her. Not while I was poling her vault, I mean; he met her the night she and I piled up the old red MG. We were both in the hospital when he showed up, although we were fine.

We never told him I creamed the side of that

9

parked truck because it's hard to drive with somebody like Mindy going down on you. Particularly when she's tickling her twitch on the gearstick.

Now she was getting married, to my father for Crissakes, and here we were in her hotel room for that last fling before she settled down to respectability as the wife of Loren P. Holliman, and—as my stepmother!

"Is that white thing your honeymoon negligee?" I asked. I stood against her, more naked than she was, rubbing her belly with my penis as I reached around her with both hands. My fingers were happily kneading the pink bowls of her rather voluptuous tail, soothing the flesh and moving slowly to trace out its firmness and intimate warmth.

"Lord no," she laughed. She reached around to play with my butt, what there is of it. I wear a size 38 long suit, when I wear a suit, and always have to have the waist and ass taken it. "I'm not *that* wicked!"

"You're pretty damned wicked, Mindy," I prodded her anus with one fingertip and grunted when she lurched and her still-brassiered breasts tried to excavate my chest.

"Let's get wickeder," she said throatily, taking it as a compliment as I'd known she would. Her teeth were clenched and her eyes alight.

"We've got all night."

"Like hell we have! I've got a big day ahead of me tomorrow!"

"Yeah, I guess. Your wedding day. But shit, Mindy—you've had practice!" My finger was lasciviously amusing itself in the deep shadowy crack between her asscheeks.

"Here now, boy, don't be snotty! Marriage is fun—you ought to try it!"

"Me? I'm still just a baby, not even thirty yet, and I've got a sac full of wild oats to sow. And who're you calling *boy!*" I ran my hands up her velvety back to her bra-strap.

"*You,* Mister Lancelot Holliman! Tomorrow I'll be Mrs. Loren P. Holliman, and you'll be my little boy!"

"Ugh. Please Mindy—I gag easily. You want to take me on your knee and lay a bedtime story on me?"

"No," she said quickly, "but I'm glad you mentioned lay and remembered that it's bedtime. Tonight I want you to ball me blind!"

Her voice was thick with a sudden urgency. Her hands grabbed my buttocks and crammed me against her until I thought my surging cock was going to deflower her navel. Which was one thing, come to think, that we'd never got around to.

I snapped the catch of her bra, which she'd put on only because I liked it. The cups dropped from the yielding firmness of her stiff-tipped tits and they popped unembarrassedly forth. Spinning her around so that her back was to me, I palmed those pretty outriders and rubbed the nipples gently with my thumbs. She moaned and sighed, then ground the milky cones and their juicily erect crests into my hands.

She moved willingly forward when I pressured her from behind. We walked that way to the bed, getting plenty of ambulatory *frottage.* I kept forc-

11

ing her forward until she climbed awkwardly onto the bed on her knees, half falling. My hands steadied her by clutching her tits.

"How'd you like to be cannibalized?" I whispered into her ear.

She quivered. "Cannibals eat people!"

"Yeahhhh," I said, dragging it out lecherously. I felt a long shudder run through her.

"Ohhh god, baby, will you quit *playing* with me!" She writhed and used the motion of her shoulders to try to punch her nipples through my palms. "No-no . . . believe it or not . . . I'd rather just . . . just get myself balled cockeyed!"

I let go one of her breasts, pulled that hand back around her, and slid it into the very warm, tight crease formed by her thighs. It loosened up fast as she got her legs apart. I ran my thumb easily up into her love canal. It was so wet it squished. I pumped my thumb rapidly up and down inside the moaning, groaning darling, and when I released her breasts with my other hand she fell weakly forward. My thumb came out of her carnal spring with a sound like pulling a foot out of quicksand. And if that doesn't sound sexy—I was there—it was.

She lay there groaning and squirming. Obviously in need. Half on and half off the bed. The long white peignoir still lay loosely over her back and her bra was half on, dangling by its shoulder straps.

"Jesus," I muttered, gripping the negligee and peeling it up her long legs and over her impudent rump, until it was a wad of softly rumpled fabric at her waist. (Her peignoir, not her ass. There was never anything rumpled about Mindy's fabulous fanny.) "You're right, to hell with eating you. A woman as much in heat as you are gets cock, fast!"

She only sighed, but I saw another of those long shivers run through her. Grabbing her hips with a little roughness, I pulled her up until she was on hands and knees on the edge of the bed. Her naked ass quivered right at crotch level.

She stirred the air with a long moan of happiness when I shoved my rod easily into her vaginal depths from behind.

The sounds she made told me eloquently how much she loved it. A groan slipped out of me, a groan of pure pleasure. I pushed harder into her clutching vulva. Already that tingling feeling was revving up in me.

The tingle. I don't mean just in the balls, the usual lustful tingling feeling of a stuffed scrotum anxious to let off its pressure. No, this was a sensation up in the belly, in the guts, and even though I'd got used to it now with Mindy, it was always a new thrill. Each time. A new surprise. Now, with my cock being so sweetly squeezed by the soft membranous folds inside her, I felt it beginning again.

I let my eyes coast down the long sleek line of her back to her neck, pale and vulnerable-looking. Her hair had slipped away to expose it and the tiny bumps of her upper vertebrae. That is still an erotic sight to me. Very. . . womanly.

She sighed and twisted before me. Soft little sounds of happiness slipped from her mouth. The hot, fleshy pressure within her eased off around my penis, she was opening up, becoming wetter and wetter inside. Feeling her hips moving in my hands, I raised my gaze from the back of her neck to the heaving rounds of her rear end. My humping body smacked them noisily, partially flattening them with each stroke.

"Oh . . . oh baby," she crooned. "I . . . I can take . . . all of that I . . . can *get!*"

The tingling sensation intensified. I began driving hard. I patted her swaying hips and tried to give her all she could take. She lurched with the rearward impact of my thrust. Her moans and gasps continued while she jerked and squirmed in a hip-juddering, tail-wagging motion until I felt it happening. Shuddering, I nuzzled into her deep in an intense release that left me kittenweak.

But not for long.

She stretched out, then rolled over, then sat up to smile at me. We kissed, fondly now, without urgency.

"You know what? I'm gonna miss you," I told her.

She sighed. "You know what? I hope to hell I don't miss you!"

"Yeah," I said, frowning a little. I squeezed her hand. "Let's go catch a shower."

We did that. We had showered together several times before, and we both dug it. *This,* I thought, spending about five minutes soaping her tits and rolling them all over her chest, *will be the last time. Our last shower together. Shit! My father's wife, for Crissakes!*

With a lot more fondling and giggling, we toweled each other. The fondling became more involved. I saw that film of rising passion sliding over her eyes, and this time I carried her to the bed. Very tenderly, I stretched her out, opened her legs—with her most willing cooperation—and pressed a long kiss onto the pursed lips of her sex. She sighed. Her thighs parted some more. Lips like soft, wet silk parted to admit my sliding tongue. I pushed it in and out of her until she was unable to be either still or quiet. She tugged at me. Kept tugging. I came up onto the bed with her, and she kept pulling until she got what she wanted: a reciprocal trade agreement. Her mouth moved in to taste my cock and balls as I was tasting her. I felt her lips press around the big knob, the sensuous swishing of her tongue over its tip. I felt it, felt it and loved it, in every nerve and pore. Heat rose in me.

Sliding my mouth up, I found her already unsheathed clitoris and closed my lips over it. She made happy noises around her mouthful of me. I sucked voraciously on that pulsing little nub until it became a taut crest of desire that twitched in my mouth. Her thighs flexed, she hunched, cried out in that beautiful voice of final rapture, and suddenly her clitoris wasn't there any more. She came and I held my mouth there until I heard that final long sigh of satisfaction, punctuated by shuddering gasps.

Then I piled onto her because I knew what she loved.

I balled her swiftly, running it in and out, in and out of that slippery climax-wet burrow, feeling that tingle rise and rise—and rise,until it was an overwhelming pressure, like an engine running inside me and overheating, overheating—then tingle burst, balls burst, my head burst—and for about a minute I would neither have noticed nor cared if the universe had burst.

If I'd known then about that damned tingle and all the trouble and anguish it was going to cost me, I'd have tied Mindy up, gagged her, and taken her off to Mexico, or worse. But I didn't know, and next day she became my stepmother.

Jesus!

CHAPTER TWO

Ever been to your father's wedding reception?

It's a groove watching people treat the old man like a kid, and watching the bride's brother from Passaic running around with a camera, playing *Life* Magazine and hassling people until he became Mister Unpopular and the Man Most Likely to be Pitched Out the Window.

After the wedding we headed 'em up and moved 'em out, over to a crowded and noisy reception in a room like a barn, except for the blood-red carpet and those long tables full of overpriced food, bottles and bottles of bourbon and Scotch and rum and gin, even more bottles of champagne, a six-pack of IPA for Uncle Bertram, and a smallish bowl of punchless punch for the oddballs.

A lot of mighty dressed-up people. Some I knew, some I didn't. That second group included relatives, too, most of them talking to each other. Not *with* each other; *to* each other, in impatient progression. They could have used a director or a speaker's wand, the way the old Greeks did. Telling one another how they hadn't seen each other since Tom's or Susie's wedding, or Gert's or Grampa's funeral. Telling one another who'd had babies and who'd had abortions, and who was sick and where and why, and complaining about taxes and their cars and wondering why Ethel's daughter Emma hadn't got herself married, she was such a nice girl, such a lovely personality. That's what they always say about the ones that aren't married. Nice girls. Such a nice personality. Except the ones whose lack of connubiality is by their own choice. They whisper about those, with eyes rolling like marbles.

Avoiding relatives as best I could, I caught a shoulder in the left arm and my right shoulder jarred an elbow pretty badly. I apologized rather perfunctorily, saw it was a male elbow, and was assaulted by a fascinating idea.

I had nearly forgotten. I was supposed to be bird-dogging. Looking for someone at least nearly as wholeheartedly addicted to plain and fancy lechery as my new stepmother. So I patted the shoulder of the jarred elbow, apologized again, and sent my gamic gaze out in search of carnal prospects.

Poor, dumb Lance; there she was, about three feet down the table! Working on a glass of champagne with one hand and a hundred or so dollars' worth of smoked oysters with the other. Looking good. Looking available. A brunette, somewhere between college graduation and age thirty, wearing a little, hippy, nice claret red dress that fit well and did nice things for her figure without shrieking about it. I moved that way.

Edging along the table until I was close, I reached for the shrimp-stuffed celery and succeeded in losing a small amount of my balance. Or so I hoped it looked. I jarred her elbow rather nicely, I thought.

"Oh damn," I said. "I am *sorry!* Here—let me wipe that off."

She gave me a look, then directed her gaze downward to the little spot of champagne on the front of her double knit dress. The spot, barely more than a spotlet really, was busily vanishing into the fabric that sheathed her left breast. A nice looking breast, stretching a nice, paler spot into the front of her dress and trailing sexy stress-lines in its wake.

"No harm done," she said without looking up at me. "If I spill anything anyplace I'd let you wipe off, Mister Holliman—I'll call."

Hmm, self-possessed wench, I thought male chauvinistically.

"Deal," I said. "How come you know me and I don't know you?"

She shrugged. "You're one of the stars of the main event. Right up front with the conjugal pair. Anybody here who doesn't know you by sight, just wasn't looking. And any single female here who doesn't know you, oughtta turn in her hunting license."

19

I grinned and bobbed her a little bow. "Any single male here who doesn't know *you,* clever person of the female variety, oughtta turn in *his* hunting license! I sure don't like being called 'Mister Holliman," though. Sure does make me feel old, when in sooth I am a mere child not yet old enough to be mis-, de-, or untrusted. Name's Lance."

"OK, Lance. I'm Carla and I'm called Sable."

"Sable?"

"Sable."

"Sable! Bless my hunting license—isn't that a small animal bearing some relationship to the well-known mink of coat and legend?"

She showed me an exasperated eye-roll. "Beats me. Sable, you see, means black. Now while I am not of that particular persuasion myself, I do have this black hair . . ."

"All right, all right. I'm sorry for the smart-stuff." I admired her glossy black hair, which was of the so-black-it-has-purple-highlights variety. "I believe you, Sable."

"That's nice. Do you still want that shrimp-dripping celery, or were you just getting to know me?"

"I can live without it, thanks," I said, thinking that perhaps I should try to serious-up our conversation a bit before I slipped and my leg came off in her hand.

"'swhat I thought. Listen, Lance, what're you going to do, now that Mindy's married to your father?"

"Call her Mom, I guess," I answered, hopefully without a vocal quaver. *Steady on, boy!*

"Ah, an issue-evader."

I had to bite: "What d'you mean, Sable?"

She lowered long, long black lashes and smoldered her just-as-black eyes at me. "You know what I mean."

I didn't bother with prevarication. I knew what she meant, and she knew I knew. "All I'm required to give is name-rank-and-serial-number," I said, coming stiffly to attention.

She grinned and poked my shirt front in the region of the navel. "O-oh-kay, then," she sighed. "I like you better in that than in morning clothes. With that mustache and swallow-tail coat, you looked like you were an Argentine ambassador, talking with Alexander Haig about how you rightfully owned the Malvinas/Falkland Islands. How'd you change so fast?"

"Dad and I have a suite here."

"Oh? Dad and—*you?*"

I chuckled. "You're right. We *did*. He has a new roommate, now."

"Yes-s-s," she purred, giving me a smoky look. "I seem to recall having noted that fact just a moment ago."

I gave up. "All right—so Mindy's been talking!"

This time Sable chuckled, a nice throaty sound. Little woman and hippy, as I said; about 5'3", dark complexioned, a bit more than a hint of aquilinity in the nose. Short hair. Looked like she might've got the part of Brando's daughter, in *The Godfather,* but not so thin. Natural eyebrows, thick; I liked them, and her daring at leaving them totally natural.

"She ha-a-a-as," she told me. "So—what're you

21

going to do? Or do I get your name, rank and serial number again?"

"I dunno." I shrugged. "Maybe ask you to ride out to the airport with me, see the honeymooners off, then dinner someplace and back here. I've got the suite for the night and it's mighty expensive not to be put to use."

"Hm, you come on pretty fast. . . . No loyalty at all to Mindy?"

"Loyalty! She's *married!* And to my father, at that!"

Sable cocked her sable capped head. "You have something against married women?"

"No, no, nothing. Some of my best friends. . . ." I broke off with a very small smile, all it merited. "You aren't one in disguise, are you?"

"Nope."

"Anyhow, ever hear a Commandment against fornication? Moses thought that was cool. It was adultery that turned him off. Fouled up things like inheritances and the like. He had a good-looking single brother, see, a guy he set up in business as a priest. Then there was ole Joshua; you know the kind of effect a uniform has on women!"

She thought about that while I nodded to a waiter who wanted to lay some champagne on me. Receiving an urgent summons, he moved hurriedly on. Champagne was definitely in season.

"Well, that's a new interpretation," Sable said, "but I see some of the logic. I think. Moses did put in a lot of time away from home, too."

". . . sweet young people discussing religion," I

heard an aged female voice mutter behind me, approvingly.

I nodded blandly, Sable-ward. "Right. Off in the hills, rapping with Adonai."

"Um." Sable sipped from her glass. "Religious talk's so dry; always makes me thirsty," she said, nearly breaking me up. Which was probably deliberate, because she said rapidly, staring straight into my eyes, "Anyhow, about that loyalty to Mindy, Lance . . . You sure she didn't er-ah wear you out last night?" The "er-ah" wasn't a stutter or a hesitation; it was something she said, like words.

"You're the kind of woman ought to get her tail thwacked, Sable," I told her equably, "and to hell with femlib. Male lib's important, too. You're a real smartass."

"Male lib?" She arched one thick black eyebrow. "You're just not used to a female—a *girl*—talking to you that way."

I thought about that, and I smiled. "You know that's probably true? OK, Carla-Sable. *But*. We shall discuss my stepmother no more."

Another of those long, thoughtful, torrid looks: study, by a woman with an apparent liberal mix of libido and intelligence. With those black eyes canopied under black lashes, *all* her looks seemed torrid.

"Right," she said. "I've got a car here. How about if I drive *you* to the airport?"

"Cool," I said, thinking that weddings were swell places to meet new people. Fathers should marry more often! "Let's mingle."

So we mingled.

A lot of people got drunk, and there was a lot more of that weddings-and funerals talk, and the inevitable drags and the inevitable business discussions. Men walking around dead, pretending to be alive, what a shame! I overheard some comments on how much hair Fred had *gained,* and some opining about Charlie; wasn't he nearly bald last time we saw him, at Mildred's—no, poor Michael's—funeral?

"Let me just meander off," I said, "so you two can talk about how I seem to have lost my ears since the last time you saw me." I lifted my glass to the narrow necktie and the stuffed calf-long dress. And their shocked expressions. I'll toast shocked expressions every time.

I gained about three feet before my Aunt Mabel latched onto me. She gushed until I was checking my jacket to see if I was oozing with it. Then she came galloping to the point; fair hurled herself on that point. She wanted to shove her daughter Helena at me. Helena. Maybe an inch shorter than my five-feet-eleven, and probably weighed sixty pounds less than my one-sixty. You know Helena. When she quit wearing a bra, she had to *tell* people. Wore sweaters for the sole purpose of keeping warm. And here she came, wearing not a sweater, but a dress that could have been picked out only by Aunt Mable.

Leaning over a little, I navigated around Aunt Mabel's overpadded shoulder so I could whisper in her ear. The big diamonds were cold against my lips.

"She *does* look like a good lay," I told Aunt Mabel, which was far more deliberate vulgarity than deliberated veracity.

Aunt Mabel assumed a position that made it appear she had been drenched suddenly in starch. Then she ushered Helena off to try someone other than the family lech. Helena glanced back at me, and I noticed for the first time what fine bone structure there was in her face; damned if she wasn't pretty. I puckered my lips at her, but turned to talk with someone before she had a chance to react. It's a mean trick.

I went back to mingling. Kissed a few relatives. (I did *not* kiss Janey, who was too willing.) Cousin Karen gave me tongue. Pretty good tongue. I hope her husband gets his share of it. If she could get close enough, around Cousin Cecil's belly. Beer and football. On TV, I mean. And Karen still had her face, most of her figure, and her yen. Christ—men! We distend and get marshmallowy *without* being stretched by babies!—and cut up women for not returning posthaste to their eighteen-year-old bods and retaining them into their forties.

Since I have got to the point of relieving myself of philosophy and personal prejudices, rather than talking about the reception, I may as well skip the rest of it.

Done, at a stroke.

We saw Dad and Mindy onto their plane with rice dribbling out of their hair, and right before he took the unblushing bride up the ramp, the old boy dropped an envelope on me. Long, white, sealed.

25

Said: HOLLIMAN IMPORT in the upper left corner.

"Wedding present," he said.

"Boy, you *are* confused," I laughed, but not until after I'd wrapped a few fingers around that envelope.

"Remember, son—you introduced me to her."

"Yeah, you girl-thievin' creep-ass," I said, and we laughed, and locked eyes for a moment, and I pocketed the envelope, and Loren P. and Aminda A. Holliman were off to Nassau.

I will not comment on my calling him "creep-ass," or my activities of the previous night, or which of us was the real McCoy.

Sable and I went back to her Corvette and started back downtown. She made me buckle up. A woman with the courage of her constrictions.

"What do you do, Sable?"

"Nothing. What do you do, Lance?"

"The same. Who are you? I mean, Carla who?"

"Carlotta Maria Magdalena Montanelli."

"Whew—hey! You mean, you're *Carlo* Montanelli's . . ."

"Right."

Carlo Montanelli was Dad's main European agent. Field Vice President: Europe. Big-nosed, ugly Italian (there are some) with a full head of beautiful white hair and mistresses in about six cities (including Rome, New York, Paris) that I knew about. Lived up in Connecticut somewhere, and traveled most of the time. I was not only surprised that Sable was his daughter, I was amazed that he had such a good-looking daughter. Also that she was so far away from being revoltingly fin-ishing-school finished.

"Where do you want to eat, Sir Lancelot?" she asked, tooling along with the expertise of a veteran Manhattan driver.

"Uh—Pavilion?"

"Closed. Where've you been?"

"Uh—is it an ethnic insult if I suggest Mama Leone's?"

She laughed. "Hardly. I've never been inside the place. Don't tell the Family—but I don't care for Italian food. It's one reason you don't find any Italian women with figures beyond the age of thirty. Or younger."

"Well—let's go back to the Hilton, have a drink, and talk about it."

"I sort of thought you'd suggest that."

"Yeah, well, I did suggest two other places."

"Uh-huh. I was afraid you'd think you had to go through a regular litany of restaurants. I suppose that airplane hangar has room service?"

"Airp—oh, the Hilton. Yeah. And dinner can be had for little more than the price of a State Dinner at the White House with Ronnie and Nancy. Would you like to be room-serviced?"

She kept her eyes on the cars ahead. Didn't even blink. "I think that's the general idea."

I reached over and gave her thigh a squeeze. That's about all you can do, in a 'vette.

"Careful. I warm up fast."

I jerked my hand back. "Drive, driver!"

She did, in silence. Plying the traffic with a cool expertise I admired. Why Dad had taken a 4:48

27

(meaning 5:23) flight I'll never know, but between five and seven PM is *not* the optimum time to navigate Manhattan.

Eyes ahead, Sable asked in that quiet voice, "Are you really as great a lover as Mindy says?"

"We agreed not to talk about Mindy anymore."

"Sorry. Are you really as great a lover as I hear tell?"

"Yeah. Dad started shoving books at me when I was fourteen or so. Maybe thirteen. Or twelve, or something. Anyhow, he thought I should know. Said he started at *eighteen,* though."

"Um. You gained carnal knowledge from a book?"

"Not *a* book. There were a lot of them, including hardcore pronography. Also, it was sort of like a college science course. You know—books and laboratory experimentation simultaneously. How old are you, Sable?" I wanted to get off the subject. Where it's at with me is not only that I am considerate and not a hawg at the planet's finest and most maligned activity, but neither am I adolescently fast at coming, nor do I have difficulty achieving orgasm. The first leaves a woman hanging in space, the second uptights both her and her grunting lover.

"Twenty-six," she answered. "How old are you?"

"Less. But I like older women."

She stared straight ahead and kept a perfectly straight face. "I know."

I guess I've neglected to mention. Dad is forty-nine, one of those young forty-nines, you know,

28

and my new stepmother Mindy is thirty-one, if all that matters. I guess it does, in a way. Talking about how Sable and I got to the hotel and Dad's, I mean, my suite, and mixed ourselves a pitcher of martinis and got all acquainted—enjoying each other's company because we're both sort of addicted to what's called clever repartee—and all warm and glowing and sexy—that doesn't matter though, does it?

We had the top of Sable's dress down and I was sucking away at one of the dark-tipped beauties she didn't insult with a brassiere, while she did a lot of sighing and wiggling and stroked her fingers lightly over the libidinous bulge in my pants. They kept getting tighter.

"I've got a confession to make, Lance." Small, quiet voice. Eyes down. Fingers busy.

I slicked my tongue over a nice, tight nipple, like a large, red-brown pearl. "You're married."

She squeezed that bulge in my fly. "No!" She chuckled, throatily.

I squeezed her other tremulous tit and licked its twin again. "You're a virgin and you want me to be gentle."

That time she laughed. "I'm not a virgin, this is a democracy without 'gentlemen,' and gentle men bore me."

I didn't say the obvious: that I planned to. I cupped her pretty dunes; squeezed them harder. "I give up. So confess."

"I'm flying the red flag."

A little chill ran through my balls, which already

29

felt as if someone had been pumping them up with air, hot. "Fine time to tell me that, witch!"

I raised my head from her acorn-shaped breasts, at the same time taking one in each hand and palpated them as if I were testing grapefruits. Women who have something to squeeze, I've noticed, seldom object to that, assuming a man doesn't play caveman or Igor.

Sable didn't object: "Uh!" She sighed and trembled, putting her dark head back on the couch. "Yep. You have a reputation, Sir Lancelot."

"He laid his best friend's wife. I'd never."

"All right then, you have a reputation, comma, Lance."

"So's your old man."

She chuckled. "You're too cocky."

"That's true."

"But—I like you. So I changed my mind. Because you say things like that—umm!"

"Like what?" I asked, lightly pinching her nipples, then tugging them out long. They didn't look like berries or buds or any of that stuff. They looked like erotically swollen nipples, and that's a good way to look. And feel.

"Like—I asked if you're a great lover and you said yes, matter-of-factly, and then you told me why. Or part of why. And just now I said you're too cocky, and you said 'That's true.' Among other things, I like that. It isn't that you're *just* an egotist. You don't have any false modesty. Egotists put me off. But false modesty's worse. Now o'erweening confidence and a complete lack of modesty, those are—irresistible."

30

"Umm. Would you believe I was ready to walk away from you, two minutes after I met you?" I admitted.

She jerked a little. "No shit!"

"As I said, you're a smartass. Then I learned that you're also smart, like intelligent, and there aren't many. Well, let's see now," I said, fondling, pressing, squeezing, tugging. "Flying the red flag, eh. Hmm. These are too small to screw."

"These" were her tits. They were very good tits, jugate jugs, and maybe they were big enough at that. But they lacked the hugeness or the flaccidity necessary to form a substitute vagina. I kneaded and mauled the pointed, high cones, which were about as yielding as softballs. Which isn't very. I let my fingers sink rather cruelly into their foam rubber softness/firmness, because she had indicated clearly that she liked a bit of bosom-mauling. My hands slid out to the tips, toyed with the nipples a moment. Then I tweaked those soft buttons until they jumped out into instant hard-ons again.

She sat there and writhed and moaned and clutched the bone in my crotch. It imitated a bone, more and more.

"It's a nice *mouth,* though," I said, kissing her.

She let me know it knew what it was doing by opening up and sucking my tongue, hard.

Retrieving my tongue, I pursued the subject of what we were going to do about her plugged twat and my twat-plugger.

"Good-looking butt on you, too, woman. How'd you like to be buggered?"

She shuddered violently that time, and her

mouth went limp on the oral digit it had again grabbed. I took that for a strong negative. Deciding she was an anal virgin, I pulled Sable up as I stood. I was thinking hard. My dick wasn't. It was just itching.

"Get those clothes off, woman. I'll finger you off."

After a shudder, she kissed my neck. "And. . . ."

"You'll suck me off."

Putting on a little show, she had her thumbs in her pantyhose when I shoved my shorts down and toed them off my feet. She paused to gaze at my hard-on with those intense black eyes. It jumped out and throbbed before me in tingling alertness, showing off and looking for more tingle. It was pointing at her, both suggestively and aggressively. Not to mention rudely.

"Umm," she said. "Now that's *pretty*. You're built to be a lover, all right." She sighed. "All right, I'll admit it. I'm damned sorry it's this time of the month."

I wrapped my hand around the base of my thick horn and shook it at her. "All swollen up and no place to go," I lamented, grooving on what she'd said.

She said she was sorry, meaning it, but she mimicked a soul-kiss in the direction of my penis. Then she peeled down her pantyhose, and I was even sorrier. Sable! Yes, and what a glossy, sleek, absolute forest of thick, jet-black hair she wore over her mounded vulva! What a mossy, lovely mat to cushion a hard-driving pelvis!

But I saw the little white cord, too, very bright amid all that coal-black foliage.

She straightened, slowly, naked and checking me for reaction. She got it. She got a stare. An all-over stare.

"You're one in a million," I told her quietly.

She cocked her head, giving me a questioning look.

"You honestly look better without clothes than with. And Christ—that beautiful Mount Etna makes me testy about what I'm missing by not getting into its heat."

She smiled and gave her head a slow nod of appreciative acknowledgement. I resolved not to mention it again.

"Come over here and give me the next best thing, woman."

The hint of a frown appeared on her face, but she came. Naked, and with a slight juddery jiggle of her tits. I waited, smiling, knowing why she had frowned. But I wanted to surprise her.

I did. When she reached me I pulled her close and kissed her gently, moving my lips only a little, moving my hands at the same time, kneading the emphatically firm flesh of her buttocks. They were more than bowls. Rounded almost-globes that swelled brashly out from the base of her spine. Her hands roamed me, too. They felt more than warm. Her breath hissed, hot on my mouth.

Then I hoisted her, crushing her to me as I lifted her with my hands under her buttocks. I carried her that way, walking carefully, into the bedroom. There I lowered her just as carefully to the bed.

Then I made her squeal: I gripped both legs and lifted them while I plunged my face deep between her thighs.

The nascent frown I had seen had come from my sort-of order, and her memory; I'd told her that I would finger her off.

I would have had to have been a one-hundred-percent complete idiot not to have known what the little string meant, so white against her pubic hair. The tampon would do its job.

I pressed my mouth to her furry mound, which was astonishingly silky, and kissed her there with firmness. Then I sent my tongue slipping through those delicate tendrils to kiss the pursed lips hiding beneath. Setting my tongue against that soft-lipped opening, I pushed it slickly inside.

"Oh," she groaned. "UH—oh . . . Jesusgod!"

I began wiggling my tongue and stabbing it in and out until she was writhing in ecstatic response. Her moans were loud. She wasn't bothering to control them. Her mounded breasts shuddered and heaved and speared their surging peaks upward.

"Ah . . . ah . . . my . . . *god!*" Your *mouth!*"

Moving upward a bit, I swirled my tongue over and around her nubby love-button until it jumped up into a quivering female hard-on. She gasped and tightened her fingers in the sheet. Her thighs flexed turbulently as she hunched, sliding her lower lips up and down on my mouth. I was careful, abandoning her clit to lick and chew on the soft pink flesh of her labia. Then right back to the lusty nubbin at the apex of those lips.

Her knees lifted. She moaned and shuddered. I

licked, pressing hard with my tongue. Her thighs gripped my face as she felt the warmth and pressure of my mouth and tongue on her most sensitive flesh.

Sable was one of those women whose sexuality is at its peak during the post-fertile period, rather than when she's in oestrus. I didn't do a thing but roll her clitoris under my tongue. She didn't do a thing but moan, and groan, and twitch, and jerk, and then come, at something like 9.9 on the Richter scale.

She drifted, then, in the warm rosy afterglow of ecstasy, which added to my happiness. Everyone knows that coming is one of the great pleasures of life; certainly not everyone knows that so is making someone else come. I lay there with my head cushioned between her thighs, enjoying the softness and warmth.

She regained her breath and her control and came after me full of love. Kissing and cooing. Squeezing my penis fiercely. Then loosening her fingers to hold it, her hand moving gently and lovingly.

"God," she sighed, "it's hard as a rock!"

We got me turned around, sitting on the edge of the bed, and then I was looking down at her shining crown, flanked by glossy black hair with purplish highlights. Her hand slid down my cock and off it, to press the slippery eggs below. I felt her breath on my glans. It made me shiver. Then her tongue. It moved softly, moistly. I shuddered when she tongued all over it, making my highly aroused sexual flesh tremble and swell while she moistened it. I closed my eyes and started getting high on head.

Then I gasped and nearly fell back when she sucked me into her face.

Stroking her hair and shoulders with trembling hands, I gasped again and again. And swallowed, hard. I opened my eyes to watch her head moving. Up and down, up and down. A naked priestess of phallic cult, on her knees before her deity—and hers was not an impotent god! Tongue, wiggling. Lips, sliding. Mouth like warm melted butter, sucking. Her head bobbed. Up and down. In and out. Her fingers clutched. One hand on my knee, the other at my ever-tightening balls. Then she was sucking. Long, hard pulls designed to pull my semen up out of my aching scrotum.

She did. I went off like a cannon, collapsed backward, and had to push and pull her face away when she continued sucking at flesh that was suddenly too hyper-sensitive even to be touched.

After awhile I sat up and pulled her up into an erect kneeling posture. Then I know that I really surprised her; I fondled and squeezed her dangling breasts with one hand and her plugged snatch and clit with the other until she came, again.

I left her on the bed, wasted, while I went in to start a warm shower. Then I looked at her from the bathroom doorway.

"Come on in."

Naked, her legs apart and her pubic bush sleekly damp, she blinked. "I—I've never been in a coed shower before."

"It's a rush. Come on, time you got your feet wet."

She laughed. "My hair. . . ."

". . . . Is short and will dry fast. Come on." I extended a hand.

She started moving. A little smile was just beginning to curve her mouth.

"And—Sable."

"Hm?" She was right there, standing short and naked and sable-haired before me, with eyes like coals ready to go from black to red heat.

"Take that thing out of yourself first, Sable."

"But—oh Lance . . ."

"*Do* it." I turned to enter the shower, so she'd know I didn't have any intention of watching. As I stepped in, I tempered that macho command: "Please."

The rushing water drowned all sound. I stood there soaking it up, really appreciating it—but wondering if she'd do it, if she were really free enough and had the strength; if she *could* do it.

She could. She did. The curtain was tugged back just a crack, and I looked at her. Poised there beautifully naked as if ready to flee. Then she smiled and came into the shower with me. We pulled the curtain back into place. We began playing around with each other's naked body, and giggling. The water rushed down onto us. It was wonderful. We made no pretense at all, but fondled and explored each other unabashedly. Up, jerk by jerk, I came.

"Ooh! Look at *you!*" she said, smiling. Yes, "unabashed" was the word for her and her approach to sexuality.

But I was even less abashed than that. She didn't consider the concept, didn't know what I was doing until I did it. Her legs were open. I was delighting her innards with my hand, liking the way the hissing water ran down her body, collected in her black fleece, soaked it, formed it into a glistening raven beard, and ran from its tip in a steady stream. Then I squatted, moved closer to her, and used one hand to open her. The other I used to guide myself into her.

Her eyes went huge. Her mouth dropped open. A throaty groan of surprise, of slight shock shuddered out—and changed into a sound of absolute delight. I think I echoed it; God, she was hot inside; I'd never felt such heat around my tool. I haven't since. It was an absolute first, for both of us, and the absolute best.

The water rushed down and splashed and hissed over us, and we hardly noticed.

With her wet, bare butt tightening in my hands and rubbing the back wall of the shower, we screwed that way, standing up in the rushing stream of water. Both of us were as if high, sliding into another reality, close to being overcome with the rapture of what we were doing—and with that weird (shameful!) feeling of delicious *wickedness* you get when you're doing something "against the rules"; rules you're proving are so much nonsense.

O lord, O Sable, but it was so hot, so slick, so good, so *good,* for us both.

Storybook time arrived; we came together, or nearly, with her tits plastered hard against me and

38

her feet off the floor and water running down onto us and off us both and her legs trying to climb mine.

After awhile, we rather weakly went about the business of soaping and rinsing. I left the shower, toweled, and went out into the other room to collect her purse and clothes. Those I left in the bathroom. Then, after checking out dinner with her, I closed the door. I called downstairs.

Sable emerged just after I'd hung up. In a jauntily disdainful, wanton gesture, she hurled her clothing into a chair.

"I don't *want* that shit!" she told me, in manner most firm. Then, "And you even thought to put my purse in there and give me privacy! What a darling, what a man!"

Trying not to look smug, I didn't say anything. She knew exactly why I'd put the purse in there. Because women always carry spares at that time of the month, and I knew she'd have to re-plug. She came over to kiss me. Then she stepped back, hugging herself and succumbing to a strong all-over tremor of reminiscence.

"How did you *ever* devise such a lovely, supersexy thing to do?"

"Please believe me: I invented it for the occasion."

She studied me, dark-eyed. "I think I'll believe you."

I nodded. It was the truth. I'd never had that sort of urge before. I hoped I would again—and with Sable or someone as un-hungup as she.

We were sort of quietly getting into each other and our experience when the food came. She giggled and returned to the bathroom. After sliding quickly into a robe, I went to admit Room Service. Red wine. An even one-hundred raw shrimp. Twenty oysters on the

39

half. A big pot of blood-red hot sauce, packed in ice. I sighed; he left. Sable emerged, clapped her hands and laughed; pointed and snapped out "Off!" and I grinned and dumped the robe.

Naked, we ate our shrimp and oysters and drank our red wine. And exchanged looks, along with a few words. Lord, that food was good! You just don't have to get fancy-pantsy about food to do something that's really fun in the way of eating!

Then that time came.

"I have to go back up to Connecticut tonight."

"*Have* to?"

She nodded, silently and sadly. "*Have* to."

"Ugh! This weekend?"

She sighed and shook her head. "Day after tomorrow Mother and I are flying to Florence, Lance. For two weeks."

"Jesus Christ!"

"Yeah." She stared into the silver bowl of hot sauce, sadly depleted. "See you later, when we get home, lover?"

"Yeah," I told her morosely.

But I had just had an ugly, nasty, even more morosifying thought. There had been one, only one thing, missing in our lovemaking. Despite the passion, the delight, the rapture, the just plain delicious *enjoyment*—no tingle.

I hadn't felt that familiar tingle I'd always known with Mindy. It was something special. I had just vastly enjoyed something special. But the tingle had not been there.

And that's when it began. Right then, with that realization. That goddam elusive tingle!

CHAPTER THREE

I was checking the Saturday Night Movies on the tube when the phone rang. I flopped back onto the propped-up pillows on the bed and picked it up. I answered. Didn't recognize the voice. Nice voice, though.

"This is, ah, Cousin Helena."

Oh yeah, the tall skinny cucumber. Helena isn't my real cousin, of course. She's Aunt Mabel's daughter, not Uncle Boyd's. Aunt Mabel's first husband is dead. So is her second: Uncle Boyd. Poor Aunt Mabel is sort of almost-family, she and Helena. That's what she's called, too, like "damyankee" in the South: Poor Aunt Mabel.

"Oh," I said, "hi, cousin. Thought you were back in Michigan by now."

"No, Mother's turned on to do some New York shopping. She also told me you are an arrogant, nasty young man and I am *never* to have anything to do with you!" Her voice was light, lilting, to let me know I wasn't to take umbrage; she was just reporting.

I laughed, non-umbrageously.

"Well?" the phone demanded of my ear.

"Well, what? You don't think Aunt Mabel would lie to her own daughter, do you?"

"Lord yes, but that's not the point. Don't you even *care?*"

"Uh-uh. No, Helena, Aunt Mabel just isn't one of those people whose opinions I give a happy shit about."

"You *do* talk nasty. But—neither do I, Lance."

I pulled the phone away from my ear and gave it a look. It just looked smugly innocent, as if it weren't saying nutty things in my ear. Oh well. I returned it to my face.

"Neither do you what, Helena? Talk nasty?"

"No," that cool voice said. "Give much of a—damn about her opinion."

"Clever girl," I said, noting her amendment and wondering if there wasn't any shit up in Michigan. Maybe not. Maybe that's why there's more snow than grass? I made a face at myself in the dresser mirror opposite the bed. You feel disconnected from life, sort of dissociated, when you're talking on the phone, mostly listening, with someone you don't give a shit about and don't even care why that someone called.

"So what did you *say* to her, Lance?"

"Oh come on, Helena. You don't want to know. It was arrogant, also nasty, and you shouldn't have anything to do with me. Hang in there with those snowy-headed Michiganders."

Silence.

I let it lengthen. The silence trick doesn't work on me. Dad taught me that. Says letting silences lie there is one of the secrets of being a good executive. Most people treat silences as women: something to be filled. But if you let silences sort of run on, growing more and more pregnant and louder and louder, you tend to learn things.

At last she broke. "Tell me."

"You won't like it, Helena."

"So? Are you too uptight to say it to my face?"

I chuckled. "I can't see your face," I reminded her.

That didn't work. "So? Are you too chicken to say it to me?"

Oh oh. Hitting me where it hurts. Right in the *macho!*

"Aunt Mabel," I said with determination, "was trying to shove us together. Very obvious about it, too. That always bugs me. In point of fact, *she* does; she puts me way off. So I whispered something nasty and arrogant in her ear. About you."

After another waiting silence that got her nothing, Helena said, "I'm listening."

"The following," I said wearily, "is an exact transcription of the words spoken about Miss Helena Holliman by Lance Holliman, well-known arrogant nasty, into the shell-like ear of Mrs. Mabel Holliman: 'She *does* look like a good lay!' "

43

This time the silence ran on even longer.

At last I said, "Helena?"

And she said, "that *was* arrogant and nasty," sounding a little uncool and she hung up.

I put the phone down, got comfortable, and skipped the unusual Saturday night Ick Flicks to watch "North To Alaska" again. It was worth it, just to see that big muddy fight at the end, particularly from the pretentious opulence of a suite at the New York Hilton.

Then I went to sleep. It had been a lot of day, and a lot of night.

In the morning I remembered what I'd forgotten, what with the distinctly distaff distraction of Sable. The envelope Dad had slipped me before he left for his and Mindy's second honeymoon—their first, together. I fished it out of my coat and used my comb to slit it open. One thing I hate, it's papercuts on my fingers.

The unsigned note said:

"Thanks for introducing us. Why don't you take a trip, too? Try not to make it a honeymoon."

He hadn't bothered signing it.

The check said:

"PAY TO THE ORDER OF LANCELOT P. HOLLIMAN—$5,000.00."

He *had* signed that one.

Good old dad, I thought smiling, and it was hard to let go of that check, even just to put it down while I went around getting ready to check out. Five thousand. Why not take a trip? Why? To get away, why else? To get away from what?

Well, er-ah-um . . . hrrrumph.

To get away to *where?*

Carla/Sable Montanelli crossed my mind, and I contemplated a trip to Florence. . . .

But why, I thought as I packed up, go chasing after the daughter of Dad's European VP, when the Montanellis would be around for years? There were, after all, so many females I *didn't* know—and never would know, either in the usual way we use that word, or in the chickenshit usage one finds in the Bible—if I didn't work on it.

Shit. There was a pair of shorts under the bed, and I'd just closed the suitcase.

And, I mused, going off to Europe to make it with a girl from Connecticut—like hauling beer to Milwaukee, I'm thinking!

Besides, the scene with Sable had been great, but dammit, that *tingle* hadn't been there. . . .

After making another last round of the suite and discovering that I seemed to have gotten everything packed, I called Dad's office, then went down for some breakfast, after telling those guys that's where I'd be. The two guys with a truck showed up when I was about halfway through my ham omelet, and I gestured them in. That dismayed both patrons and servants in that so-fancy dining room. I enjoyed their dismay. The two guys were dressed in those gray uniforms Sears sells, matching pants and shirts. Both shirts said *Holliman Imports* across the back, and the slender black's left shirt pocket advised that he was Roger. The redhead with the belly had "Ike" on the tab of his pocket.

45

"I've got a lot of stuff to move, but let's have a coffee first," I said.

They looked around nervously, whereupon everyone who'd been eyeing them swiftly shifted gazes elsewhere. We got that coffee, too, all around; although the hotel servant acted a bit stiff. Catch 'em arguing with Loren P. Holliman's son, though!

Roger and Ike were pretty uncomfortable, sort of strangers in a strange land, but I knew they were both enjoying hell out of it. They didn't do much more than respond when I talked about the boss' being married and so on, and how the joint would probably go to hell while he was down in Nassau honeymooning.

Eventually we finished off my breakfast and their coffee, and they tailed me up to the suite, bearing a couple of big boxes. I had already packed all the clothing: now we went after everything else except the contents of the refrigerator and the partial bottle of Beefeater's and another, hardly touched, of Hennessey's. Let the housekeeper and maids work that out between them. The rest of the hooch we packed into the moving boxes.

I'd have preferred using the regular elevators, but the truck was parked outside near the service elevator, so we hauled our stuff down on it and loaded up. Dad had already laid a large chunk of money on the Hilton, and I didn't worry about the rest of it; they'd be happy to bill us at the office address. Or maybe Dad had credit carded it and signed an untallied bill. It didn't matter. Ike and Roger and I drove off, heading for the house out on Long Island.

Riding in the big Holliman Imports truck with those two cats was fun, if a little crowded up front. They talked a lot more easily, out of the hostile environment of the hotel dining room.

We pulled up behind the big house and started carting in all that stuff, under the watchful supervision of Martha. Martha had been with the family at least as long as I have, a WASP who, like Shirley Booth, could play a Jewish mother to perfection. She has the dumpling figure for it, too.

Ike and Roger put up only brief and token resistance to accepting the pasteboard box full of assorted booze. They left happy.

I told Martha no, I didn't want anything to eat, and no, not even a doughnut or a slice of küchen, and no, I really don't want to eat anything, nothing at all, honestly Martha DAMMIT, and yes, coffee would be nice. That made her happy. With both Dad and me gone, Martha would be best advised to import some male into the house, just so she'd have someone to hassle—I mean serve. It's mighty hard to believe in the Just God concept when a woman like Martha had been widowed in her twenties and never got asked again.

"You had a phone call," she said, bustlingly fixing me a cup of coffee as if it were a five-course meal at the very least.

"When? Today, you mean?" I was scanning the paper. It said the usual. Same thing it said yesterday, but with rearranged paragraphs.

"About twenty minutes ago."

"Oh. Who was it, Marth?"

She advised that the caller had left no name; female gender. After setting my coffee in front of me—there was too much milk in it, but I wasn't about to ruin Martha's entire day by mentioning it—she found her note.

"You're to call back," she said, placing the little torn-off piece of paper beside me. "Waldorf, room four-twenty-six. You sure you wouldn't like a nice piece of that apple kooka?" Which was the nearest she'd ever come to pronouncing küchen.

"Absolutely don't need it, thanks. I had orange juice, a big, lovely, yellow ham omelet, coffee, and an entire piece of toasted bread," I told her, knowing she'd be mollified at the news that I had eaten well, had taken care of myself, *with* butter. There was a B etched into the pat, so I suppose it really was butter."

She looked a little nervous. "How—was the omelet?"

It had been surprisingly good, but here was my second opportunity to ruin her day, by saying so. So I gave her a look and said, "Oh come *on,* Martha! It was hotel food!"

That brightened her up. She nodded knowingly and in false sympathy while she ran her hands up and down her aproned thighs. (I guess she takes off the apron when she goes to bed. Otherwise I never see her without it, except on Sundays—but that's not Martha. That dolled-up, corseted creature who emerges from her room every Sunday morning to go to church is someone else altogether, in a not-so-clever plastic disguise that somewhat resembles Martha Hirschberger.)

48

"I gather I'm to return this call," I said, studying the tiny piece of paper as I waggled it.

She nodded. "I'm sorry I didn't get the name. You don't know who it might be? You haven't any idea? I wonder who calls a young bachelor so early in the morning?"

It was ten minutes to noon, but I saw no reason to mention that. It *was* morning, and Martha would have just told me so.

"Well," I said, picking up the coffee and leaving the saucer, "I know how to find out."

"You're going to call back!"

"Martha, you're psychic."

Her plump face glowed with a pleased smile and she glanced at the kitchen wall phone. Hopefully. I gave her a Look and went through the house and up to my room. I heard her sigh. But one thing about Martha we were sure of. She was so good and so conscientious about her eavesdropping as to be almost of professional rank, but she drew the line at picking up an extension and listening in. That was too easy. It was not a part of her code, her special ethic of eavesdropping.

In my room, I called the tired old Waldorf and asked for room four-twenty-six.

"Hello?"

"Hello. This is Lance Holliman, returning a call to someone there who failed to leave his or her name rank and serial number."

"It was me, Lance."

"Oh." I recognized the voice. "That's 'I,' Cousin Helena."

She ignored the deliberate nasty-arrogance. "I

called the Hilton and just missed you."

So one assumes, I thought, and I said, "All right," How stupid we are to say "Oh, I'm sorry" under such circumstances, and think we have to make excuses, and start telling our business to a voice on the phone! Besides, being sorry to have missed Helena's call wasn't my thing. Had I been in love with her or something, I'd have *had* to say I was sorry; that's part of lovers' mutual regard. But not being in love is never having to say you're sorry.

I waited.

"Are you planning to come back to town, Lance?"

"God no. Manhattan's for tourists and editors."

"Not—not even for me, Lance?"

"Wha-a-a-at?"

She didn't sound cucumber cool. She sounded soft and cuddly, and not too expert in that role: "I mean after all, I *do* look like a good lay. . .?" She practically whispered that last word.

I sighed. "Helena, I only said that to shock Aunt Mabel."

Silence. "You—then you—you mean I *don't.*
. . ."

I didn't answer. No, not to me she didn't. Most of all, Helena was Aunt Mabel's daughter. And she looked like it, too. But also—too tall, and not enough meat on her. I don't go for the model type, or the Tab-soda-girl type, or all those skinny Nordic-accented semi-females who used to try to peddle me stuff on TV.

I think it was right then that I decided to go to

Italy after all, and find me a big pasta-fed *Italiana,* with big strong thighs to provide pillows, and big strong calves to squeeze a man half to death.

After the usual silence that was a staple item, already a tradition, in our telephone conversations, Helena said:

"You—arrogant *bas*tard!"

She said it very nicely and succinctly, too.

"Click," I said, playing Criswell.

"*Click,*" the telephone said in my ear, putting me in the prediction racket.

I cradled the phone, drank off the rest of my cool coffee, and went back downstairs. Martha had the television on, and looked guilty, of course. Martha would vote for Nixon from his resignation to the end of the century, if possible.

"Martha, I don't *expect* any, but I want you to know that I am *not* taking any calls from a Miss Helena Holliman. And you are henceforth to get the name of anyone who calls here, not just the room number."

Muffin-faced Martha nodded, wearing an expression of mingled guilt and almost comical dolorousness. "And what," she asked quietly, "should I tell Miss Helena Holliman, should she call?"

"Tell her I have the clap."

Martha nodded solemnly. "Yes, Mister Lance."

I laughed and gave her bigole soft shoulders a hug. "You keep on calling me 'Mister Lance,' young lady, and I'm gonna start calling you 'Mis Marthy,' " I threatened.

She nodded with a little smile. "Oh, my! It's af-

51

ter twelve! What can I fix for lunch?

I finally settled for the goddamned küchen. I think she was afraid it would spoil. Martha should have been in Secretary of the Treasury Regan's spot, not to mention taking over for David Stock-man, the Budget Director. And I can assure you that she would have kept her mouth shut when the magazines came a-calling for interviews.

The kuchen wasn't quite stale, yet.

CHAPTER FOUR

"No-no," Rafaela Tambroni said, accentuating her positive enunciation of the negative by shaking her wealth of red-glinting, dark brown hair. It swirled in a beautiful thick veil about her face and shoulders. "No. I will not put my mouth on you, and you will not so do to me. Is understood?"

Capisco, I assured her. I'd have had to be possessed of the sensitivity of a Chicago politician, not to mention illiterate in two languages, to have failed to understand her. "But ah—why, Rafaela?" I asked, regarding the vision of Latin pulchritude adorning the center of my hotel room.

She drew herself up, gaining an inch or so, and the liquid green of her eyes seemed to go all cold and hard, like jade. "To do so is wicked!"

Well, that was that. You're in a hotel room, about to make it with a superbly endowed and presumably willing female of the opposite sex, a big pasta-fed girl of nineteen, or twenty, with big, strong pillowy-looking thighs, mostly displayed below her abbreviated skirt, and big strong calves to squeeze a man half to death. You *don't* start saying things like "sententious." Or any other sort of put-down. I sighed.

"But—okay, doll," I muttered. Damned Pope! What's he got against oragenitalism anyhow, particularly when it's a *prelude* to his mandated begetting activity? I sighed again, gazing at her.

Rafaela. I'd met her just a few hours ago in a noisy, smoky disco on the Via Speranza. That's a street in Rome, which is really Roma, and which is in Italy—which is really Italia. A's and o's are very big over there. Yeah, Rome. Not Florence, where Sable presumably was. I went to Rome.

Rafaela. A healthy-looking Roman, well-fed and glowing, with a big wide mouth made for the fellatio she denied herself—and me—and an unconditionally Italianate nose, strong chin with a dimple, green eyes that seemed backed by flame, and a magnificent mane or ripply, shimmery dark hair, all full of red and copper highlights. Hips like venus. And a grandoise bosom. Its halves were grandiosely displayed in—and out of— a print silk dress that seemed angry at her amazing breasts, and was trying to spew them up over its scooped "neckline" like jiggly spumoni.

She'd been fantastic on the dance floor, fantastic sitting across the little round table from me after we sort of picked each other up. (There didn't happen to be anyone wiggling in front of her while she was dancing, so I filled the gap. Instant friendship.) Leaning enthusiastically forward over the table, shadowing it with her bust, she'd been a vision of Italian warmth. Her green eyes on mine, locked, full of fire and daring and, I thought, promise. Mine trying to stay on hers, rather than take the big warm dive into Grand Canyon.

We got along. She did what came naturally when she danced, and I've always made up my "steps" as I go along, just doing whatever the body feels like doing in some accord with the music. A bit of thoroughly insane dancing, a couple of drinks, and here we were, after two AM, in my room at the Hotel Roma. I wasn't wondering what Martha was doing back home, with both her menfolk in absentia.

And—as the lady said, *nessuno cunnilungo, nessuno fellatio!*

Rafaela was a liberated Italian girl. Meaning she would ball. But that's all. Oh well. Lots of guys have wives of the same unfortunate persuasion, I'm told.

I smiled at her, getting ready to break up the impasse by crossing a few feet of blood-red carpet to pull her close in a musicless *Danse Erotique*.

"Voi Americani!" You are so *oral!"* she said, with a separate gesture for each word, regardless of the language.

But then she was spilling her big, tasty tits out (I had tried one in the taxi) as she hauled her dress down. Her manner was a businesslike one that

55

would have scared the load out of the standard, sit-com-watching American husband. The effect on me was a bit different; my pants got tighter. My tailor had cut them according to the fact that I "dress right," that is I wear my cock 'n' balls to starboard of my fly. Not now. Now I was dressing straight up the middle while Rafaela undressed.

That, she accomplished with impressive rapidity and ease.

She was the kind of woman who looked as if she had gone back to the breast department for seconds. (Do you know that the Italian word for "mother" is mamma? Does that maybe look to you like the singular of mammae, meaning mammaries, meaning jugs? Does that tell you where it's at with Italian women? Liberated hell—mothers go through life being called "Tit!")

"Don't be an ugly Italian," I said, joining her in undressing.

"HA!" Loudly. "You KNOW I am not!" Rafaela's dress did a complete nosedive to crumple forlornly at the base of her tall and fully developed body. She turned slowly, as if on a pedestal, all tan and pink and very naked. No stockings, no panties, no nothing; she hadn't worn a damned thing under that flippy little dress! And I'd thought she'd been wearing some sort of push-up shelf bra under it. After all, there'd been little sag and no sign of nipples poking out the silk from inside. She had her own built-in Merry Widow bra!

She completed her 360-degree turn to face me once again, erect and almost nipple-less tits bracing me. "I am a *bella Italiana,* no?"

"Si," I sighed, and speeded up my efforts to render myself sans shorts. Due to the extreme swelling of their sheltered burden, those briefs were damned hard to get off, close onto painful. My straining, hard-beating penis was a turgid rammer, pulsing anxiously for the rammee.

"Ahhh," Rafaela commented with respectful appreciation and a cock-lover's glowing eyes as she eyed my liberated quarterstaff. "Is a good cock, Lance! Is a pussy-pleaser, I can see that!"

Parting her legs, she put both hands down between big columnal thighs to peel open the richly-fleeced lips of her gash. I admired the violently red inner labes and the dark damp hole beyond.

"Come put heem een, *innamorato mio!*"

I went to her with alacrity, naked, standing erection bobbing before me like a battle standard. We were both barefoot, and she was looking into my eyes with no more than five degrees of tilt to her lovely chin. A big woman. A tall woman. Big hips, solid and well-padded under my hands. Brashly jutting buttocks, resisting the indenting efforts of my fingers as I pulled her to me, braising her belly with my manhood.

I felt her radiant warmth, seemingly rolling out to me in gusts.

Her hands went possessively and assertively to the same portion of my anatomy. She clamped my ass with all eight fingers and both thumbs. Then her big tits were trying to maintain their bold front against my chest, threatening to keep our mouths apart, as our hands dragged each other close. We were prevented from some sort of strange fleshly

57

melding only by the standing hot poker and the two big outriders between us. Our mouths came together like a couple of furnaces. Hers opened sexily and moistly, in imitation of that humid-lipped lower mouth. Each of us began trying to prove his own tongue was longest. (It's a bad language, English. Using the word "his" with reference to any portion of Rafaela Tambroni is not only ludicrous, but obscene.)

I began moving, and she began backing, and then I heard the splatting sound as the smooth, clearly-defined halves of her juicily-rounded rearend smacked the wall and tried to flatten out against the fuzzy wallpaper. I held her there and kept kissing her deep while she moaned and squirmed. Her every sinew was alive and amove with erotic purpose and promise. Her grinding hips rubbed me strongly with the dark-furred knoll of her crotch. At the same time she was jerking her shoulders to grind the straining, jutting masses of her tits over my chest until their pink tips seemed to burn into me. Her mouth opened wider and moved harshly against mine, sighing into it even as she thrust in her tongue and wiggled it like a restless snake's.

It was very easy, and a great surprise to her. I kept kissing her, pressing her against the wall holding her there with one hand and being clutched in return by both of hers. My other hand crept meanwhile between us—no easy feat—and I got my fingers wrapped around my thick erection. Then I began bending my knees, lowering myself, lower and lower—until I shivered at the feel of the profusely-growing tendrils of her pubic hair against the so-sensitive head of my prong. I moved a little, searching, and my cockhead discovered what it sought, the slit of her puckered and parting quim.

She gasped when I started straightening. Her eyes went wider and wider. So did her humid vulvar slash. I shoved up and in, boring upward into her as we stood there, feeling the moist warmth of her inner circle all around my tool.

"Ah—ahhh, you wicked man. You—you screw me standing up!"

The only brilliant answer I was capable of was a smile; that standing entry into her warmth and startling tightness was almost excruciating.

"M-mos-s-st-ah!—men are not tall enough to do this—ummmmm!—with Raf-Rafaela," she gasped, hunching now, grinding, sliding her tight slot down my up-pressing pole, her eyes rolling as if they'd come loose from their muscles.

It isn't that I'm all that tall, of course, at five eleven. The thing about it was that Rafaela was little less than an inch, or an inch and a half, shorter. The number of men in America that are her size is low enough, and in Italy, men tend to be a bit shorter. I was thoroughly delighted that I had chosen to do something that pleased her so much! I admit to going up on tiptoes, then. I had implanted myself far up inside her, and now I was able to look down at the spraddle-legged girl's face from an even greater height.

"Rafaela," I said, grinding my crotch against hers and my chest over her breasts in two separate motions, "is just a *little* girl!"

A great smile made her face seem to glow and she clutched me tightly, at the same time wriggling and gyrating with more enthusiasm than she had displayed on the dance floor of the disco. "Ah! Ah! What a lovely thing to say!"

I started scrubbing her bottom over the wall in a frenzy of gyrating thrusts, crushing her big, solid jugs under my chest, and goading her to an even more frenzied response by ramming way up inside her. All my energy was centered in my groin; driving and goading her with the thick mass of my dick. Her nipples had appeared, blooming pinkly like shy night-flowers.

And wearing myself out. A standing screw is not really my forte, despite the pleasantness of the change. It's a posture for athletes. My legs start jumping with weary tension very quickly. They did so even faster with Rafaela, because she was responding in a way that had our bodies slapping together with loud smacks and jarring force.

But just as I was about to suggest that we adjourn to that piece of furniture normally thought of in relation to the relations we were having, she gasped, grunted, shot out both hands to grab my hips and buttocks in viselike grips, and came!

It hadn't really occurred to me that her clitoris was getting all that much attention. Or maybe it was the excitement, the novelty; some of us make it faster than others, and with more ease.

But to hell with the analysis. That big woman was writhing and gasping in an obviously excruciating grasp of climax, and orgasm so violent that I could *feel* the series of violent spasms in her creaming quish.

Then she was weak, sweating, sagging. Getting her to the bed, dammit, was *work*. She collapsed heavily and weakly, and I was quickly made aware that she wanted to—had to—rest for a few moments. Rest was not my bag at that time; my penis was jerking convulsively and uncontrollably, full of lust and need.

Then she wanted me inside her again, and she was almost desperate in her grabbing of me, throwing her legs lewdly wide, hunching hard to screw herself on the big penile shaft she held at the base with her own hand. I was happy to sink down between her legs onto her pillowing, billowing breasts, and into her silky-smooth snatch. Winding her legs around my hips, she smiled, and sighed, and began hunching and jerking. The head of my cock banged around against orgasm-wet vaginal walls and sank deep to scour the whole intensely hot inner cavern of her.

That was a wild fuck, and an unforgettable one. The extreme heat and constriction of her torrid cleft was like none other. Her enthusiasm, aided by her strength, transcended even Mindy's.

I seemed to come forever, and I lay there groaning as I did, fantasizing that I was pumping about a gallon of me into her, squirting like milk from a cow's tight-squeezed teat.

I was still lying atop her, spent and gasping, when she went to sleep.

I was still lying atop her, too, when I joined her in what used to be called the arms of Morpheus.

61

Strange how Venus and Morpheus so often go hand in glove, isn't it?

Yes, I know. I haven't mentioned that old tingle.

I haven't mentioned it becaue it wasn't there with Rafaela.

We woke in the morning, and gazed at each other fondly, and in short order our bodies were united again. And it was good again, better than good.

But—no tingle.

I still lay on the bed, wondering about it, when she emerged from my bathroom, after her shower. She bent for her dress. I watched as she slipped the little silk concoction on, jerked her head to rearrange her hair, and was presumably ready to go about whatever her day's business was. But I didn't smile. I was wondering. Worried.

Rafaela came and bent to kiss me. I palmed and stroked as much of her big silk-clad, almost nippleless breasts as my hands could encompass. She broke the kiss, stroked my face fondly, and straightened. And left, without a word.

I wondered if she'd be back at the disco tonight. I also wondered what if I showed up again; would I be ignored? Was she searching, the same as I was? I didn't know, and I knew I wouldn't find out. I wasn't over here to try and work up a courtship, to fall in love. I was over here to get the hell away from Mindy, and New York, and the memory of the tingle she had given me, every time—and to try to find that elusive sensation again, somewhere else. With *someone* else.

I was beginning to know something approaching horror and fear, and I jumped out of bed and practically ran into the bathroom to shower, to get it out of my head.

But it persisted, that ugly thought.

Did that marvelous tingle exist for me only with—my father's wife?

CHAPTER FIVE

I had decided against staying at the Excelsior, which is a hotel that rings, and bustles, and positively jingles with over-moneyed actors and new-rich Americans who don't know how to handle either themselves or their money. Instead, I was farther down the same street at the tired old Pinciana. It's named that because it stands near the gate in the ancient red brick wall, erected long centuries ago against the possibility of *Barbar* invasion; the Pincian Gate, admitting now into the coolth of the shrubs and tall pines of the Borghese Gardens.

I awoke there my second morning in Rome, in a rumpled mess of a bed, the thick linen spread dragging the floor, the thicker velvet drapes holding the morning sunlight at bay. I lay there awhile and thought about Rafaela—and me—shaking my head.

No tingle, I thought. Jesus Christ, what a ridiculous situation! Me in Rome, money in my pocket, cock shot down and smelling like woman, wearing a little crusty film of dried semen—and me not happy with the world! *Oh no. I'm still on a Jason's quest. But not for something sensible and practical like a golden fleece, but for—a sensation I define as a tingle! A feeling! An elusive, indescribable. . . .*

Yeah, baby, I told myself as I swung my legs over, *but once you've been there, you've gotta find the way back! And not with Mindy. . . . Not with my supersexy stepmamma!*

So I got myself into shape to greet the world outside—a world of suntanned priests, mainly, and tourists and loose-bra'd Italiana—and ate the poor excuse for a breakfast the little man with the sad eyes ushered in without apparent embarrassment. One of the two rolls had raisins in—raisins that chewed as if they'd been cut out of an old inner tube. Cool coffee isn't my thing, either.

"Tomorrow," I said, "one will refuse rolls with raisins in. You will bring me no rolls with raisins, and the coffee will be hot or your ears will be."

The sad-faced man spread his hands without changing expression. "It is of a piece," he said.

"What?"

"Si," he said, and departed.

I was still reflecting upon his morning-talk awhile later as I rode majestically down in the open, gilded cage of an elevator and crossed the lobby. I don't need much breakfast, don't take much, but I thought it would be nice to go out and find something. A cup of coffee made with coffee, perhaps, and water that was at least warm. A roll that wouldn't dent the floor if dropped.

A couple of Americans, nominally female with their bodies gusseted and their hair worn like enormous birds' nests stiffened and sheened by lacquer, were babbling away together about something, and they asked me if I could help.

"No spikka d'Inglis," I said, with a smile and a lot of head-bobbing, and I went on.

"There you are, Sally. See? What they told us was a lot of baloney! There went *another* handsome Italian—and he didn't pinch us either!"

Probably bruise my fingers on the girdles, I thought, ambling along the broad promenade named Via Vittorio Veneto and called simply Via Veneto. The sidewalk was dappled, if not darkened, shaded by closely-planted trees, and amid the bird sounds were those of many voices, mostly speaking another language. That is still an odd feeling, to walk among people who *look* OK, you know—you don't *rook rike* foreigners—and yet to hear them chattering away in a language you once studied and thought you could speak and understand. . . . If only you had been taught that they talk so fast and slurrily. It would be interesting to be a foreigner for a few minutes, somehow, through hypnotism maybe, and to be able to hear Amerenglish as a foreign language. I suppose it sounds fast and slurry, too. Like getting a Brooklyn cabdriver in Manhattan.

66

It's a lovely broad avenue, the Via Veneto, astonishingly short when you think about all it contains and about how well-known it is. I walked happily past the little church, past white-uniformed policemen who actually change the traffic lights by hand, past milling tourists and tits-out young Romans, all amid the cough and put-put, and roar and screech of Vespas and Fiats and tourist-buses. A young priest gunned past, handling his Vespa like a New York cabby, riding it like a black-skirted cowboy, broad-brimmed hat and all. His exhaust stank like that of the vehicles of the more worldly.

(More wordly? He was probably connected with the Vatican, I mused. No parish. Parish priests in Rome are peons. Everybody who is anybody is on some sort of Vatican duty, running errands for the Pope, or one of the army of cassocked old men *il Papa* surrounds himself with. In which case, my Vespa-straddling priest was just as worldy as that idiot Texican coming out of the Excelsior in his eleven-gallon hat and his blond boots—and with his loud mouth and a wallet as bottomless as his oil wells!)

Poetic on this sunny morning on the Via V. V., aren't we, I thought, and started across the street toward the mostly-tourist cafe—what else, on the same street with the American Embassy and the Excelsior?

That's when I nearly got myself run over by the yellow Fiat.

Its driver bombarded me with bilingual insults as he swung and shifted and gunned along the broad expanse of street. I stood there quivering in after-

67

shock; his machine had actually touched my trousers, and now when I looked down at the pale gray double knits, I saw a smudge of oily dirt.

"Shit."

A clear, tinkle-belling voice laughed, and a throaty but high-voiced Italian accent asked, in English: "Is that all? You could have been killed. Just—*shit?*"

The word sounds better, pronounced "sheet."

I looked at her. Sitting in a wicker chair before the little sidewalk table, shaded by the cafe's awning. Shaded further by a broad white hat with a bright, broad silk band of purple and yellow and green. Wearing an off-white dress that looked like it had cost her—or someone—a bit of money; you don't find such plain, no-nonsense, undecorated little frocks in cheap stores. Her lily was ungilded. And so were her legs, about a yard of them, encased in hose only a bit darker than her flesh. Lots and lots of leg. Her gams seemed all over the sidewalk, even though they were arranged in that demure way you learn in finishing schools.

"My apology, Signora," I began, dragging my gaze from her superb calves at last, and not without a struggle with intransigent eye muscles.

"Signorina," she corrected, with a high-voiced chuckle. A throaty, high-voiced chuckle; can you hear it? It's a lovely sound. Girlish and very womanly, all at once.

"I'm sorry, *Signorina*," I began again, trying now to see what sort of face there was, in a sort of semi-hiding beneath the *baldacchino* of her white floppy hat. It had teeth, I saw, quite a number of

68

them, and they were bared whitely in a smile. "But I . . ."

"If it is the word you are apologizing for, Signore, I will not accept. It was a natural enough reaction. I, myself, might well have said 'shit' under such circumstances. Permit me to apologize for the driving of my countryman."

I gave her a weak smile. There was still that empty feeling in the gut, the wriggly feeling, and my legs were beginning to quiver.

"Perhaps the Signore had best sit down," she said helpfully, "before he falls down."

I glanced around. There were no tables, and I kind of like to do my own picking up. But my legs put up a stout argument. They would be, they advised me without equivocation, most happy to assume a different posture and to cease supporting me. Or else.

I thanked her and sat down. She glanced up, made a gesture, then looked at me, leaning close, shadowed by hat and awning.

"You *are* all right?"

I nodded. "I am fine, Signorina. Thank you very much. I seem to have gotten a bit dirty, that's all."

She reached over and touched my leg with her white-gloved hand. Long fingers. "Umm, the American double knit. It washes like hose, no? No problem—but is that not a snag?"

"Double knit snags if you look at it," I said. "It's the American way. We come up with a fabric that never needs ironing, that doesn't even need to be hung up, the perfect traveling clothes—and we feel a little guilty about it. Perhaps such perfection might interfere with the GNP. So we build in a fatal flaw." I touched my double-knitted leg. "In this case, a fabric that is menaced by so much as a hangnail."

She laughed. "A bad case for double knit," she said, "and a bad case for America." I saw that she had a fine, long Italian nose, a chin that was almost but not quite pointed—and equipped with a fascinating dimple—and a very wide mouth. Also a lot of high and highly prominent cheekbones. One of those chiseled faces, but carved by an artist, not an artisan. He had known what he was doing, and he had done it with some care and pride.

A waiter had materialized at my elbow.

"Cinzana," she told him.

"Coffee," I said.

"No no, the wine is for you."

"Thank you Signorina, but I don't want any wine this time of day." I wished I hadn't added the last phrase; it sounded terribly American and a bit put-down-y.

"But—coffee? I should think the automobile was enough of a stimulant."

"Ah. . . ." the waiter was standing there with his head swiveling back and forth as if it were mounted on gimbals. Little man; big mustache. His expression waxed bleaker and bleaker.

"A coffee," I said, "and a nice little roll, please."

"A brandy?" she offered, still trying.

I gave her a tiny smile, then twisted my head slightly to look up at that poor waiter. *"Caffe,"* I said firmly enough, and he looked grateful, glanced a bit nervously at her, licked his lips, looked at me again, and departed.

"You are forceful," she said.

"Just in more need of coffee and a decent roll than wine," I said, "distilled or not. But thank you for thinking."

She nodded and sat back. I saw that she was nursing a little glass of wine. A large white purse of monk's cloth lay on the table with the straps dangling. My eyes dropped to her legs, automatically, but I hoisted them up again.

"My legs make you nervous?"

I blinked. "Ah—nervous," I said, waving a hand. "Or—something like that, anyhow."

She laughed. She laughed easily, and a great deal. "You are a tourist?"

"I suppose. I'm wandering. My father just got married, for the second time, I mean," I added hastily, "and before he went off on his honeymoon he handed me a large check and suggested I wander, too. I am wandering."

She smiled, and nodded. "Wandering. Is a good thing to do. You are, ah, 'doing Italy?' "

"Please don't put me in that class of tourist," I said. "Oh—and my name is Lance Holliman."

"Lance Holliman."

I nodded. *"Si."* If she wasn't into exchanging names this week, I wasn't about to pressure her.

"Your father is rich, then?"

I smiled rather diffidently. "Damn, another cliche—I guess so, though. I guess I'm one more rich American."

"But you are not staying at the Excelsior."

I shook my head. "Too many rich Americans," I told her, and we chuckled together. "I'm at the Pinciana."

"Ah. I am Constanza. Hello, Lance."

"*Ciao,* Constanza," I said, and the waiter was back, with coffee and a large and pleasantly soft-looking breakfast bun.

"Anything else, Signore?" he asked, and when I had shaken my head, he looked at her. "Contessa?"

"No, thank you."

I was staring at her, naturally enough, as he went away, and she merely sat there smiling at me.

"You are incognita," I said.

Another laugh, of course, and a wave of her white-gloved hand. "I saw no reason to give you a title. You gave me none."

"We don't have titles in America."

"Oh? The members of your parliament are called 'The Honorable,' and ministers of flocks other than Catholic are called 'Reverend,' as if it were a noun rather than an adjective, and I have met a Kentucky Colonel, too."

Unable to avoid laughing at that last one, I nodded. "I stand corrected, Contessa." And was I ever to remember this little exchange about titles and money, later.

She pushed back her hat a bit, letting me see a pair of clear blue eyes. "Constanza," she corrected. "Connie, even."

"Connie, then. But let me hear the rest of it. We Americans are so impressionable."

After a moment, she said, "Constanza, La Contessa di Stresa."

I raised my eyebrows, and after a moment she asked, "Are you impressed?"

"Of course. It also has a lovely sound, you know. Contessa di Stresa."

"It is better than *di Strega*," she said, making a small joke; *strega* means witch. "But I am impressed, too. With the handsome son of a wealthy American—who does not stay at the Hotel Excelsior."

I toasted her with my coffee. She lifted her wineglass to me in a return gesture, but barely touched it to her lips. My coffee was cold. . . .

"What are you going to do today, Lance Holliman?"

I shrugged. "Get hit by cars and talk with beautiful women."

"What a *gallant!*" she cried delightfully, but with a smile to show me her head wasn't really turned. "But you are not planning to gain an audience with Pope John-Paul the Second, or see St. Peter's, or stare up at the ceiling of the Sistine Chapel?"

"St. Peter's might be interesting," I said, "just because it's so big. And I guess I would not mind seeing the Pope at all. He seems to be a truly wondrous individual, and an inspiration to millions. But no, I have no need of staring up at Michelangelo's ceiling; I've seen a thousand pictures, and the movie, too."

So we were getting along fine, and one thing led to another, and she drove me to St. Peter's, which is ridiculously immense, comparable only to the Vehicle Assembly Building at Cape Canaveral, and she told me the story of the fisherman who saved the obelisk by shouting out that the ropes should be wetted; they were starting to stretch as Sixtus the Fifth oversaw the thing's replacement. Its weight was some 300 tons, but wetting the ropes did the trick, and the fisherman's family had had a monopoly on providing palms to the Vatican, ever since.

"Your family?" I asked Connie, and she laughed, telling me no-no, her family's glory had begun under the Borgia Pope, and "you know what *that* means, Lance."

Well, I didn't, but I figured the first recipient of the Stresa title had been a bit of a boot-licker or worse, and we didn't go into that. We wandered a bit, with me getting shown some stores I mightn't have got into, and ate at a tiny place, the name of which I never remember without consulting my matchbooks. And she drove me around in her car, which was a thirteen-year-old Oldsmobile. A miracle; I never knew there was such a thing as an American automobile looking and operating so well after the usual three-year lifetime built in by Detroit to coincide with the period of the usual bank loan.

Constanza insisted on taking me home with her.

We arrived in the late afternoon, and a uniformed woman advised that Connie's parents were out. Castel Stresa was that, a castle, and nicely situated, too. It also looked not only as if it had seen better days, but had very nearly forgotten them. The place was coming apart at the seams—

among other places. A great pile of old stone, nearly obliterated by convoluted vines like green serpents. But the paintings and furniture, and silver and crystal and other glass looked as if they'd have supported a dozen rakes all the days of their wastrel lives. Constanza took me on a tour, which terminated somehow in a bedroom like something you've seen in movies; massive standing wardrobes and chairs, an enormous bed canopied under white and sky blue, leaded windows, tall and arched, and a truly magnificent chandelier. Other appurtenances, or perhaps impertinences, were her own additions: a nice little lamp with a moving shade, surrounding colored bulbs, a stereo and several Moody Blues albums, among other things, and other modern thises-and-thats.

"Lovely," I said, for the umpteenth time. "I have seen many rooms, Constanza—but you haven't called any of them *the* guest room." We were standing in the approximate center of her bedroom, holding hands. She still wore the gloves.

She turned to me with a strange little look, eyebrows up. "But this is it. Do you not want to sleep here?"

Conversation languished.

Now look, I could have said something dummy like "But where are you going to sleep, Contessa," or even "With *you???*" as if too-too surprised, shocked, and delighted. Or I could have said "Sure baby," and leered. Or I could have—never mind. What I did was tighten my hand on hers, pull a little, and get a lot of long slim Constanza, la Contessa di Stresa, right up against me.

She kissed damned well. She kissed as if it were going out of style and she was determined to get in her innings first. Her mouth parted swiftly, and while her hands went scurrying over my back, she waggled her tongue frantically over mine, which was busy, too.

The kiss escalated in fervor and intensity. I moved my lips on hers, tripping my tongue in and out of her moist and tremulous mouth. I did not taste the wine there, because we had both drunk some, but I liked the raspberry of her thinly-applied lipstick. Meanwhile, she crushed herself to me, squashing her tits against my chest and clutching with all eight fingers and both thumbs. My pants started getting uncomfortably tight and the kiss grew increasingly more intense. My hands wandered.

Her dress zipped up the back. It zipped down the back, too, and fell nicely away to give me a pleasant surprise. What I had thought were nothing much turned out to be small breasts, yes, but very firm and beautifully shaped. The fact that I had been with her all this time and not known she wore no bra is a clear indication of the firmness of those lovely cones. Being faked out by bra-less women was beginning to become habit for me.

The dress went on down, with ease. She was very slim indeed, stomachless and almost hipless, long and slimmer of thigh than we are conditioned to think is good. Her panties were tiny, silky, and not-quite transparent. But the ball of fur showed through, and . . .

I have neglected to say that Constanza was a

76

blonde, a darkish, ashy blonde, who wore her hair drawn up and twisted a time or two and then pinned neatly. With pale eyebrows, thin ones, and blue eyes. Regretful oversight.

She was unbuttoning and unbuckling and unzipping me while I ran my hands over her nylon—maybe it was silk—sheathed buttocks and down her thighs, and in to caress the bulge where her full bush pressed irrepressibly against her little panties. The bush was obviously blonde, too, and I was glad. It isn't that I've got much against women who become two-toned when their pubes are bared, but she was *so* blonde that it would have been a shame to have been suddenly faced with a big forest of brown or black or something.

I glanced around, losing my shorts to her ardent hands. "Servants," I muttered, "parents. . . ." The door into the corridor was open.

"Forget them, forget them—ummm," she murmured, the last little hum of appreciation elicited by the baring of my bodkin, which was standing up and squaring its shoulders as she relieved me of my shorts.

"One of us better—ah—close—uh—the door," I muttered, glancing again in that direction and jerking a little while her hands wandered and did interesting things to my cock and balls. She still wore the white gloves. Neither of us had gotten around to them. Since the almost-flesh-colored hose were held up by a white satin garter belt that was decorative and would certainly not get in the way, I saw no reason to remove them, either.

Then she was striding, not prancing, or dancing,

or swaying, but striding, in manner most business-like and unaffected, to the door. I admiringly watched the roll and up-and-down piston and bunch of her buttocks as she walked from me. It was a cute little ass, cheeks like bowls set closely together, looking no larger than the span of my hands. But I already knew that they were *slightly* larger; my hands had been exploring those pretty cheeks with their pretty peach-cleft. They felt good, so firm as to be almost hard. And they looked good, too.

So did her long body, her nice handsized breasts hardly jiggling in their muscular firmness and jut, her blonde-furred vulva seeming to wink at me as, after closing but not securing the door, she returned smiling to me with a gait only a little less businesslike.

This time her body came against mine hand-first, so that she cupped my livid organ with her palm, cupped my balls with her fingers, even as she plastered her tits to my lower chest and her lips to my mouth and started moving both, humming and sighing.

But my dear countess, I thought, *I hardly know you!* And I held a firm asscheek in each hand and strained her to me. Both her cool arms were around my neck, now, and my hair was hopefully passing the white-glove test of commercials gone by.

"Umm, you have such lovely *hair,*" she sighed, squirming nicely.

"Umm, you have such nice *everything,*" I responded brilliantly, rolling an eye at the bed to gauge its distance.

We made it.

We flopped on that great four-poster bed, pulling and tugging at each other, hunching and sighing and groaning as if both of us hadn't had sexual release for months. I heard the bed groan, too, as I eased myself quickly up between her widespread thighs and thrust between her soft labia with one swift lunge, pushing them aside and doubling them in with the excited thickness of my shaft.

Overexcited, I'd forgotten that I hadn't touched her pretty tits; for all I knew she was dry inside or had to have her orgasm first, manually or orally, or liked to surmount, or preferred a long foreplay, or—whatever. Instead, here I was acting like a damned American on his honeymoon, ramming and cramming straight into her without more than the brief fondling we'd already done.

It didn't matter. Despite the sudden, almost beserker force of my entry, the way was easy. I went into her, all the way, and she was both wet and open. I lay there a long while and just luxuriated in the marvelous sensation of it, the hot wet feeling of twat all around my twitching throbber, which was pounding away inside her like a fat man's heart.

Then, propped on my palms laid flat beside her head, I raised my body off hers and stared down at her. Her eyes were bright, her mouth open, her nostrils flaring with each breath. Her expression was loving, not put off by the sudden near-rapelike entry. Nevertheless, I pulled all the way out, slowly and loving every second of her inner flesh sliding wetly along my organ, pulling and easing back until I had cleared the gaping damp lips completely.

She gasped. Her eyes flared widely. Her hands grabbed me. "Put that back!"

I put it back fast, sending every inch rapidly rushing back through delicate inner tissues, and she moved with me, screwing the deep hollow of her belly up onto my phallus.

"Ahhh," she groaned throatily, but the bed was making more noise. Groaning. The overhead canopy rustling. I've never made it in such a noisy bed.

Her hands clamped me, tightly. This time she was being absolutely certain that I didn't get away! "That feels so goo-ood in me!"

"Oh, sweetheart," I told her in a strained voice, "is *that* ever a mutual feeling!"

She wiggled. The bed creaked. "And now—move, my darling, move, lover, move, move!"

I moved. Up and down, back and forth. And the bed groaned and creaked until I was nervous about it. But she didn't seem to be, and I continued those ancient movements.

My hands pressed her long slim form as I pressed my nakedness strongly against hers. I could feel every muscle, way down deep inside her quivering slit. They tensed and pulled around my organ, and they grew wetter and wetter in her excitement. Rolling her hips, that tall slim woman grasped and tugged and pulled, pushed and swung, getting it all, all of it, way up inside her in a way that made us both gasp and shudder because it was so damned good.

The bed complained. I tried to ignore it and concentrate on *feeling*.

I could imagine that I felt that thick, tubelike ridge that ran up the ventral surface of my penis swelling, growing more and more huge. I stroked it in and out of her, and then got a little rough, making my belly and crotch slap hers, making the bed sound like a house caught in a high gale.

And she only grinned and gripped me tighter.

She was gobbling me up now into the hot moist interior of her as thrills of passion sizzled through both of us. Deliberately teasing, I pulled far back. She had nothing left inside her but the bloated knob of my cock. I hesitated a moment, watching her writhe in an obviously uncontrollable desire to swallow me up until my glans teased her deep-seated cervix. Then I began moving my hips back and forth, moving on and in her gently, still teasing, while I watched her eyes grow larger and larger, becoming huge and shining and fixed, like great blue marbles set in her face.

And she came. I could *see* that wave of pure ecstasy sweep her, rush through her. Then I was feeling the swelling, pulsating waves that ran through her vaginal chamber in an all-pervasive consummation of her passion, which was apparently as easily sated as it was ignited.

The bed complained loudly when she began tossing herself about once more in cheerfully licentious activity.

Obviously she wanted me to begin moving again, at once. I did, at last falling upon her full length with all my weight and gathering up her round little asscheeks in my hands, probing and plunging deep into an orgasm-wet slash to the accompaniment of noises from that damned old bed that I was sure could be heard in downtown Rome. If that was the case, people minded their business; nobody responded. Constanza did, very nicely. She responded with some brilliant and rather complicated movements of her own, so that we had the bed going several ways at once. It griped, but went creakingly, groaningly along.

Very little time passed before I was groaning and shivering, growing all stiff, and she was taking my seed in writhing, grinding, grinning gratitude.

At precisely that moment, the goddam bed gave up the ghost and collapsed with a great crash.

CHAPTER SIX

I don't recommend it.

Having the bed cave in just as you come, I mean.

Particularly a canopied bed. Particularly in a strange hou—excuse me, castle. Particularly when you're at your weakest. Particularly when you don't even know your partner-in-sex. Particularly when you don't know anything about her daddy, or his views on her balling with American pickups from the Via Veneto, or whether she has one or seventeen brothers who may be armed with mighty fists and steely thews. Or guns. Or just mean faces; lord, at the moment or orgasm, I couldn't fight off a smallish platoon of cockroaches. Or the Egyptian air force, even.

It was the foot of the bed that gave way, not the

head, so that we were propped, our heads about three feet higher than out feet—it was a very old bed, and high off the floor. Fortunately, the canopy held. Its curtains merely slipped their moorings and slid shut, gliding downhill toward our feet, shutting us off very nicely.

"Jesus," I said, or something like that.

She began laughing. "Why not 'shit?' " she suggested.

"That,too," I groaned, feeling myself sliding backward off her perspiration-slick body, feeling my depleted worm of a cock start easing out of her.

She sighed, trying to hang onto me, and beginning to slide herself. The head of the bed retreated in the distance, which increased. "It *always* does that," she lamented quietly, but she giggled.

Somehow that made me laugh, too. We laughed together—like idiots, naked, sweaty, comey, supposedly exhausted. Sliding backward down the ramp her bed had become. Hanging onto each other. And laughing.

It was all so funny, and then so hilarious, that we kept laughing even after I devised the idea of rolling sidewise, so that we both rolled nakedly out onto the floor with multiple thumps and a few extra grunts. We had shared something, and it was both funny and nice, that godawful incident, and pretty soon we were sort of messing around again, still giggling now and again. Pretty soon I had a soft-on, which is to say it was long and thick, though not hard, and I was amusing myself—and her—by running my hand up and down over her right breast, forcing that stiff projection to flop in spite of its determined musculature. Then she was scrambling around, and that's when I learned that she was not only a perfectly wild lay, but damned good head, too.

It was so good I didn't even think about the tingle, It wasn't there. I did her with my hand while she sucked and bobbed her head. My finger prodded, probed, and slid into her. I found a slippery, hot, and seemingly liquid hole. It moved, or rather she moved it, so that her sex slot locked stubbornly on my hand, on my doubled fingers, and when I drew them out of her vagina's tight-lipped wetness there was a sound like the popping of a wine cork. Groaning, she kept on sucking and bobbing her head over my now-hardened tool, all the while twitching and jerking with convulsive contractions of her entire body.

I began rubbing and rolling the nice little lump of her clitoris with those same two fingers, lubricated from her own inner front. Her pretty lips clutched and clung to my prong and slithered along the shaft almost in desperation as my hand on her trigger began to raise her higher and higher toward Climax Mountain.

Then she couldn't hang on anymore, couldn't concentrate on what she was doing because of what was being done to her. Groaning and sighing, she fell back and lay twitching as if in pain, hunching her gloriously bare crotch to my hand until she came again, and her hand came rushing down to move mine away from flesh that was wet and suddenly over-sensitized with her new orgasm.

After a while she returned to my cock,

which had become a bit limp.

"That's all right," I said, stroking her hair, soft and blonde and coming apart from its pins. "I can save it."

She gave me a bedazzling smile and crawled half over me to give me her lips. We fell back, kissing and writhing, and if someone hadn't knocked rather diffidently at the big paneled door, I suppose I'd have been in her again, this time from beneath.

"I'm all right," she called. "I was exercising, and the damned bed fell in again!" She lay full length on me, our genitals rubbing each other happily, her nipples just touching me. I had one hand on her butt. I had frozen. The hand, that is.

"The Contessa is all right?" inquired a female voice. Accent. I mean, the Italian sounded different. Not a Roman, but someone from Tuscany or Sicily or whatever. I supposed it was a maid or some such.

"The Contessa is fine," Constanza said clearly. *"Ciao,* Gianna."

Gianna, presumably, bugged off. Constanza grinned down at me, gave her hips a little twitch, and then turned my arm to inspect my watch. She sighed.

"We must get dressed for dinner."

"Ummm—maybe we should go out. I don't know if I'm up to facing your parents."

She chuckled, at the same time slipping her hand in between the pelves. "You," she assured me, "are up for anything!"

I answered that only by rolling my eyes. Suddenly I felt a little embarrassed, or something approaching it; now we had to get up and face each other, a couple of naked strangers, and me with a hard-on up to here.

But she raised herself, first to her haunches astride me, and then to her feet. So long as she was not embarrassed about the little shining trickle down her inner thigh, I mused, I could not be concerned about my standing erection. Or embarrassment. Or our being strangers.

She stepped away. "They will not be home tonight," Constanza told me. "They are away. We will eat alone. We are all alone in this big old castle. Isn't that wonderful?"

"Alone?" What about that voice outside the door?"

"Gianna! Ha! There are always servants. But one is still alone. I mean *two* are still alone, darling Lance—with your *darling* lance. Come, get up now, and you may have a bath."

So I got up. I surveyed the bed, grinning, and of course that thinking of something other than her and sex soon had my penis back into a less demanding state again.

"How do we fix this?" I asked.

"Carlo will do it, as soon as we have vacated the bedroom. Come."

With visions of someone named Carlo sitting right outside the door, waiting to get at that no-good bed, I followed the willowy length of her naked back and good legs to her bathroom. It had been added, of course, doubtless at great expense, and at least a hundred years ago. But it was a bath-*suite,* with roomlets for various activities. That

87

way we both had our baths simultaneously. When I emerged from the shower, I toweled and then walked right past where she lay in the tub, without looking at her.

"Hmp!" she hmped after me. "Ignore me, will you? We shall see about *that*—later!"

I smiled without turning back; I was willing to see about that, later. But come to think, I was hungry. I shook my head, getting into my clothes. Jesus, what a day! And it was only seven-thirty or so, which is early for dinner, among the Italians. Dinner tends to be a project that occupies all the prime time, and God knows what they do about TV; I never learned. I was too busy being part of the programming. Gone far in delicious depravity, I was.

Thinking that Constanza would be emerging stark naked while I was now clothed, I had a sudden attack of sensitivity. I opened one of the enormous wardrobes, which I was surprised to find contained very little clothing; blouses and skirts and some shoes. I closed it and went to another. Here was a similar situation; not nearly enough wearables to fill the thing up, and I noted that they all bore store labels. Meaning she bought her clothes rather than had them made. *Odd,* I thought, *for a countess!*

But I did find a fleecy, rather utilitarian robe of deep blue. That I took to the bathroom, knocked, opened the door, and dropped inside without looking. What a gentleman!

She thought so, too, and gave me a kiss for the gesture when at last she emerged. While she dressed, I stood gazing out a window at a hillside just beautifully full of trees and vines.

"I'm hardly dressed for dinner," I said, without turning. "Particularly in a castle."

"So I noticed," she said, "but after all there's just us. Here now, stop being such a propah gentleman, and turn and see if this doesn't abet the situation somewhat."

I turned. And smiled. What a doll; she had put the very same dress back on, rather than show me up or make me feel ill at ease, in my sport coat and (smudged) pants!

"I really like you," I told her.

"Well, I should hope," she said, dimpling beautifully.

After a hug and another kiss, we emerged from the bedroom and descended the long staircase just as if we were properly dressed for dinner in Castel Stresa, which was served by candlelight, by the uniformed woman who'd admitted us, not a man as I'd expected. Nor was it as fancy as I'd expected; a perfectly good but not pretentious Valpolicella, drunk in crystal goblets along with veal tetrazzini and more pasta than necessary.

The table was very old and very long, but we got together at one end and got acquainted with each other while our legs renewed their acquaintance. The servant, whose name was Gianna and who weighed about one-eighty at perhaps five-four, was silent and seemed never to look up. I thought about her remark, that despite servants we would be all alone; I had thought it a bit of aristocratic arrogance meaning that servants were not, after all, people, and that one was alone in their presence. Maybe not. We *were* alone! Gianna was a ghost that floated silently in and out, now and again, putting and taking with never the sound of clanking dish or spoon or fork. An *un*person, which was sort of ugly. I like to talk with waiters and waitresses in restaurants and bars, joke, bring them out. But I did not say anything to Gianna, other than to answer questions; I was sure that attempting to converse would have been *just* gauche, and would have embarrassed her more than Constanza.

"It would be *super,* as you Americans say," Constanza told me as we finished off with a peach and a bit of brandy, "if you sort of wandered along the hall to the guest room I'll show you, later on." She smiled wide-mouthedly. "Much later on."

"It would be *super* if I went back to my hotel."

"Do you want to?"

"No."

"Then do not; neither do I want you to."

"OK, I'll head on over to the guest room, later. Your American is very good, by the way."

"Thank you. I have worked many hours at it."

"Why do you sit in the little cafe near the Excelsior?"

She gave me a long gaze, then blinked. I had the feeling I shouldn't have asked. At last she said, "Americans are—fascinating. I like to watch them. It is something to do," she added with a shrug, and addressed herself to her snifter.

Something to do, I thought. *So that's what the aristocrats do over here. Look for something to do.* In America, where aristocracy means money, and money brings instant aristocracy, they enter politics. My father had already mentioned it to me, a time or two. But for all I knew, her father was in Parliament, and his daughter after all, a countess, couldn't take a job as a shopgirl!

"What does you father do, Constanza?"

"Call me Connie, I like the sound of it. He . . ." She waved a hand. "He does things with oil. Olive oil, I mean. You know."

I didn't, but didn't pursue it. We tried to get inside each other's head for a while, and I learned not very interesting or enlightening things about her schooling and her Aunt Edda. But the conversation kept coming back to me, and Dad, and the business, and where we lived and how. I decided she was more interested in America then I was in Italy, and so I allowed myself to be led. As I'd said, I really liked her. I told her some stories. And we had some more brandy, and we went up so that she could show me the guest room to which I would repair—later—and then we went into her room. And to bed, and a good time was had by all. Fantastic head she gave, with that wide mouth of hers and her supreme willingness. Eventually I got down to the guest room, where I crawled into another oversized bed.

Oh, yes. Her bed was repaired when we returned to it. And it held up, that time. I hadn't seen Carlo, but he was a competent *un*person, indeed.

OK, so the tingle wasn't there. But Constanza di Stresa and I were great in bed, happy little sex animals, and I liked her, and I stayed. Sort of keeping one bridge unburned, I left my luggage at the Hotel Pinciana, but she and I went down the next day and she waited while I packed my overnight bag with this and that.

But eventually I began to piece the puzzle together, to see the light, as the old expression goes.

First there were her parents. They reminded me of the Duke and Duchess of Windsor, but in a dark Italian way. Tall and thin, both of them. Impeccable in manners and in attire. Ascetic of face, careful of speech, and sad of eyes. Strange. The feeling I got was that they didn't really *live* there in that castle that had first belonged to Giacomo Bordigo, after he had been created Conti di Stresa by the Lord Rodrigo de Lancol y Borja; Pope Alexander VI. For having knocked someone off, I think. The Borgia Pope was like that, and Cesare and Lucrezia didn't do *all* his dirty work; he had far too much for those two to handle it alone.

They welcomed me, Constanza's parents. Not with any overdone enthusiasm, but also not with any indication that they knew I was sleeping with her, which they did. At times I felt like a character in a vampire movie. Only Connie and I were alive, while with us at that long table in that great echoic castle of a bygone era sat a pair of dead people who were capable of speech and movement: the Undead. And Gianna, mobile but silent, and barely mobile of features.

But the Count and Countess did eat, and sip wine, so that I was not unduly worried about my neck. I began to be worried about something else though.

They were of the Italian nobility. Their ancestors had owned this castle, and these lands, and God knows how many people for centuries. And because that's where it's at in Europe, they were still deferred to, respected, treated with respect. *That* they had in common with nobility throughout most of Europe, even Germany, for one hears titles still in the country Hitler tried to make safe for totalitarianism in the same way Napoleon had France: by first preaching equality and doing away with all inherited titles. And the Count and Countess of Stresa had something else in common with all those other tired, inbred nobles, too. They were afflicted with an ignominious impecuniousness. Which is to say:

They were broke.

This came to me slowly. First there was the food; it was fine, and it was always there, but it was never fancy and there was never any sort of spread that would yield much in the way of leftovers. Then there were the lights; I noted that they weren't much used. The clue from Connie's room came back to me, eventually: she had enough clothes to get by, and nothing in her wardrobe seemed particularly new. There was the way she had manipulated our conversations: later, as her parents did, I realized that is was neither me nor my country they were really interested in—it was the Holliman treasury!

My country's founders, who overthrew their lordly masters and declared independence with pen and sword, immediately tried to persuade George Washington to allow himself to be called Lord!

The good man refused. But our fascination with titles and the old concept of nobility, as if merit came from what your daddy or great-great-granddaddy was, continue to fascinate us. Americans, making money and becoming the nearest thing we have to aristocratic trappings. It's all much the same as the way Hefner seeks acceptance and respectability through bringing to his magazine names with titles: from academia and government, senators and Ph.D's as though their articles are somehow better than those by the more knowledgeable—and more competent in the craft of writing.

It all began to come together in the early part of this century. *Nouveau riche* Yanks wanted titles, connections with ancient aristocracy. And Europe's ancient aristocracy wanted, needed money!

Undoubtedly it was a big turn-on to both families when Consuelo Vanderbilt, daughter of American money, married the Most Noble Charles Richard John, son of the Duke of Marborough. The reasons for the marriage were in the contract they signed, not in the loving looks they did or did not give each other:

"Whereas, a marriage is intended between the said Duke of Marborough and the said Consuelo Vanderbilt—the sum of two-million-five-hundred-thousand dollars in fifty-thousand shares of the Beech Creek Railway Company, on which an annual payment of four percent is guaranteed by the New York Central Railroad Company, is transferred this day to the trustees. And shall, during the joint lives of the said Duke of Marborough, Consuelo Vanderbilt, pay the income of the said sum of two-million-five-hundred-thousand dollars, unto the said Duke of Marborough for life. . . ."

And four percent, *said income* came to a cool hundred-thousand a year, and in those days you got to *keep* that kind of money. Consuelo's daddy had bought a title. Chuck Dick John's daddy had traded the title for yankee dollars. And everyone, presumably, was happy.

"It was good to feel sure one belonged to the American nobility," was the way Frederick Lewis Allen put it in his book *The Big Change*. That book, along with John dos Passos' *U.S.A.*, taught me most of what I needed to know about why our country is so damned screwed up these days.

So—from Consuelo to Constanza. From the Vanderbilt billion, or whatever it was, to my father's—well, it's less than a million, but he's working on rounding it off. From Connie to Connie. And "my" Connie's parents, once they learned I was from some wealth, withdrew in what I assumed was their blessing: "Screw away, daughter dear, and perhaps we can swap away the young Americano a title for the money to patch up this joint."

It took me awhile to realize what was going down in that castle—aside from Connie, who did it so well—but when I did, I started getting a bad case of itchy feet.

It was marvy, but I wasn't interested in marrying a title—and I wasn't interested in marrying without that tingle I was looking for, either. Crusades have been waged for lesser reasons, believe it or not. A lot of men lost their lives looking for an old cup, a "grail," supposedly used by Jesus at the Last Supper. I didn't propose to lose my life, but I had decided that I was willing to spend it, if necessary, in quest of that elusive tingle that made sex with Mindy the finest and most satisfying of my life.

Oh, one last point. There was no Carlo. There was one servant, Gianna. And the Conti and Contessa hadn't been gone, at all. It was the old count himself who slipped in and repaired the bed, whilst his daughter and I ate alone at his so-long table.

And damn, I really like her!

Vampires.

I have to admit it, though, whether it makes me a bastard or not, I didn't hesitate to enjoy one last fling with Connie di Stresa before I split—secretly, like an un-thief in the night. (Thieves break in. I broke *out*.) I thought I had it coming.

She was beautiful above me, long and slim and naked, coming down slowly, lowering her soft, damp loins onto my groin, opening her slim thighs wider and wider to force her parted labia down over my upstanding cock, pressing firmly and steadily to get every inch of the Holliman tool up inside herself.

I lay beneath her on my back, smiling and watching the ripple of her tiny belly's firm muscles as little waves of delight flipped through her. Then she started moving, and still I watched in delight; now her thighs tensed and quivered and her calves leaped into bold muscular display while she thrust herself up and down and up and down, skewering herself on me fast and hot.

After being still as long as I could, I began jerking and bucking beneath the enthusiastic girl, doing my best to wiggle my hard penis amorously inside the hot clasp of her love-tunnel. My ears picked up a sound I love, and transferred it straight into my scrotum: the juicy sexy sound of slapping bodies. I jerked up and down, plowing deeper and deeper into her and listening to the beautiful sensuous grunts that came from deep in her quaking belly.

My hands went up after her taut tits, almost on full automatic. I did what I had learned she liked; I clamped the resilient woman-flesh and clamped it hard. She threw back her head with a gasping groan. In my grip, her strangely girlish breasts became tight-clutched ovals rather than cones. Their tips swiftly became thick and fruity, stabbing outward between my fingers. I pushed, suddenly, with a finger against each nipple. That brought a sudden squeal from her lips, and her hand rushed down to her loins. While I pushed those thickened crests back into the yielding contours of her breasts, she began rubbing her own twitchy clit, at the same time maintaining her steady up-and-down riding of my flagpole-imitating manhood.

In a few seconds she was sighing and making tiny squealing noises; a few seconds after that she was groaning in orgasm.

It was then I tipped her sidewise, and over onto her side, and then onto her back, without losing my penile beachhead inside her spasming loins. Determined to screw her, if not to death at least into a dead sleep, I started pounding as if I were determined to nail her to the bed with my hard-on. I could feel her heart slamming fiercely against me, making the softening, relaxing, molded flesh of her bosom wiggle and seem to caress my chest.

Her hands were all over me, rushing like restless white spiders. Sighs and moans and wordless noises of both appreciation and encouragement dribbled from a mouth she couldn't get closed. I wasn't trying to come; I was trying to set a new record for *not* coming. My plan called for a soft, utterly relaxed and totally sated Constanza.

Besides, it was fun.

There came the time, as it always does, when I couldn't hold back any longer. By that time even that slim woman was covered with sweat, and I made her interior even wetter.

"Ah God," she breathed, sighing, panting, twitching her head back and forth with her hair plastered to her sweaty forehead. "Ah God, my lover—we're *made* for each other!"

I petted her and sagged gratefully, needing the total still relaxation of post-orgasm. But thinking, with what I think was appropriate Machiavellian callousness: *Right. Made for each other. Your run-down castle and empty treasury and the Holliman money. Right, Connie. Made for each other. As you'd have been "made for each other" with any other moneyed American you'd have managed to pick up—lurking as you were outside the Excelsior!*

Of *course* that's what she was doing there!

Well, she went to sleep as I'd known she would, and both my body and brain wanted to join her. But I knew I couldn't. I had to vanish, with my overnight bag, via the vines growing up the outside of the castle's walls. It was agony. First I got myself ready, me and case over at the tall pointy window, and then I had to get the damned thing open. It made some noise as I unlatched it and swung it slowly outward, and I froze. But the naked woman untidily adorning the tangled bed only snoozed on. I'd been here three days; I knew how well she slept. We'd hit the wine pretty hard, too. Or she had, and she'd *thought* I had.

I looked down and began to have second thoughts. Maybe being Count di Stresa someday wasn't so bad—the ground was a long way down, and the moon was tired, down in its last quarter, and there was a cloud or three up there keeping it company.

Again I was reminded of the vampire analogy, and this time I remembered that shivery passage in Stoker's book; old Jonathan Harker watching out *his* high castle window whilst that other Count, equally in need as the di Stresa lord, departed on his arrant errand. Climbing down the castle wall. Head-down. Gazing downward I wished I could emulate that sort of acrobatic activity.

No way! I threw my coat out and watched it flutter and swoop, coming open and parachutishly catching air beneath it. Eventually, it alighted on the distant ground with some grace. Next, I started to toss my bag after it, when I remembered the after-shave. In a glass container. I paused long enough to open the bag and take out the Brut—and to make the somnolent Connie a present of it. Something to remember me by.

I hope she'd been taking her pill.

Then down went my overnight bag: *crump!* And then down went Lance, shakily, scared half to death, hugging the vines and the stone wall beneath, thinking that Fairbanks and Flynn—or their stunt men—must have been in better condition than I. My foot slipped. My hand slipped. Once I was hanging by my quivering hands, my feet treading air as they searched desperately for some sort of perch. They found it, but another time a vine came loose and I barked the hell out of my knee and one elbow against the side of the castle. Hours seemed to pass.

But blessed be that vine! It was the only stable attribute of the whole damned castle!

It took me a long time, that dizzying downward defection, and my heart engaged in a creditable imitation of a trip hammer. But I made it, naturally falling the last few feet. I don't mind admitting that I didn't get up for a while. That ground felt good. I hugged it. Hello there, ground. I love you. Friends forever. Hang onto me, ground. I think the world's spinning, and I don't want to get off. And don't tell the Pope, he'll deny it for sure!

At last I assumed a vertical position, gave Castel di Stresa a last look, and set off hiking, carrying my rumpled case and wearing snagged pants and a shirt that looked like something I'd found on a football field, after scrimmage. Castel di Stresa loomed intimidatingly high into the night sky, turrets like fingers stretching up to scratch the undersides of the dark clouds.

"*Ciao,* vampire," I muttered, and hiked.

A couple of hours later, dead tired but feeling rather like a man stepping out of prison, I also departed Roma. By that time I was entertaining rather fond thoughts of Connie; you know how it is. But I kept reminding myself of that one essential detail that had been missing from our lovemaking. You know. The titillative tingle.

When I fell asleep on the rattly train, I was beginning to have second thoughts about my hasty decision not to ball my mother.

CHAPTER SEVEN

Florence is a word that comes from old Latin, meaning flowery. It's also the name of a tiny town in Kentucky, a town of about six-thousand people and, one hopes, some flowers. There's another, with twenty-five or thirty-thousand people in South Carolina; I think most of the flowers there are those that bloom atop tobacco plants every year. Down in Alabama there's another Florence, with thirty-two thousand or so souls—or that many people, anyhow; I can't speak for their souls. Alabama is a state I would leave and never admit having come from, but then I'm from New York and still live there, so what do I know?

There isn't any city named Florence in Italy. Foreigners just think there is. There is a *Firenze,* capital of Tuscany, which is chianti country up on the Arno. I say "up" because Firenze—all right then, Florence—is up North of Rome; *way up* North, on that godawful train I took in my precipitate flight. Think of Rome as being at about midshin on the Italian boot, and Florence on up higher toward the knee. The population must be about a half million, I guess, and you've heard of the Ponte Vecchio, an old covered bridge across the Arno where you stumble over aromatic little leather-goods and jewelry shops while you're trying to get from one side to the other; most of Florence sprawls out over on the right bank.

Florence flew pretty high, once. The gold florin was a respected coin you could find all over Europe, a reminder of the City of Trade, of the enormous banking houses of Bardi and Peruzzi, who loaned money to princes, to kings, even to emperors. Then there were the Medici. Everyone has heard of the Medici, like the Borgias. The Medici lived over Florence way. And they *ran* it. Lorenzo de' Medici—*il magnifico*—died the same year Columbus set sail for what the poor clown thought was the East Indies. Thus did Columbus help save Italy from Mussolini! After Lorenzo the Magnificent came Savonarola, another well-known fellow, who mixed church and state without seeming to realize that that was OK only for popes. They tortured him in the Piazza della Signoria—where I enjoyed a nice little breakfast at about noon, the day after I left Rome—and they hanged him there, and they burned him there, too. A little later, there came to office the man whose name became an adjective: Machiavelli. He was the nice guy who said that you shouldn't have confederates at all in your dirty dealings—which he assumed as a matter of course, as a fact of intelligent life—but that if you just had to have help, you should knock them off once the deed was done. A lot later, during World War II, there were some fantastic and bloody battles up in the Florentine hills, and right down in the Florentine streets: Italian resistance fighters against German soldiers.

Now it's a repository for a lot of art, and it has its pollution and its traffic problems. Florence isn't just wine and straw hats and tourist trade anymore. Now there are chemical plants and metallurgy, food processing plants, and other air- and water-foulers.

Up on the hills that ring the city is an assortment of historical monuments, and some mighty fancy villas. It was to one of the fancier ones that I betook myself, having decided to drop in and say hi to Sable Montanelli and her mother; I needed the company of real people, rather than the Undead.

Tough luck. Mamma Montanelli, who was a surprisingly well preserved woman with a Rubensly ripe figure and hardly enough mustache to speak of, advised that Sable was not on the premises. She was over on the coast. Well, over *off* the coast; she'd gone for a bit of a sail on some noblewoman's yacht.

This bit of news Mamma Montanelli chattily laid on me in the patio—I guess that should be "atrium" of the villa where she was staying with some friends, the Fanfanis. In relatively short order I met two or three monkey-suited servants, then Count Girolamo Fanfani, who was a tall and rugged-looking man with a magnificent shock of black hair, graying on the sides and precisely down the middle, and a ferocious *banditti* mustache that had no gray in it at all. Next I was introduced, with a reminder that I was the son of the boss of Miz Montanelli's husband, to the countess: Elisabetta Fanfani. She was not tall and she was not rugged-looking. She had a body like her namesake, Burton's ex-wife, the actress. By that I mean yeah, she was huge in the superstructure and pretty well rounded in the hips, butt, and gut, too. Her face was so slender, her eyes and mouth so beautiful, that somehow that great falcate hook of a super-Italianate nose of hers just added to the fascination and general attractiveness.

"Carla," she said in a deep voice, referring to Sable, "will soon be back, Signore Holliman. Meanwhile, you must stay with us here." She flashed me a magnificent and almost blinding smile; blinding both because of the true whiteness of her teeth—and the two gold ones I saw inside.

"I . . ."

"Carlo will show you to a room," her husband said in his own forceful, if tenor voice, "and dinner will be at half-past-eight. Cocktails . . ." he smiled and made a beautiful gesture with both hands. "Any time. Officially at seven-thirty."

"I . . ." *OK,* I decided, *let's try this living-in business again. There doesn't seem to be a husband hunting, money-hungry junior Contessa on the premises!* My—luggage. . . ."

"Paolo will take care of that; he'll fetch your things up in the car," Count Girolamo said. "Where are you staying?"

I chuckled. "I spent most of the night on the train from Rome," I said. "But I've checked in at the *Gonfalon*. . . ."

"Good," he said, nodding briskly. "Unless you wish to return to town this afternoon, Paolo will drive down, obtain your bags from the hotel, and that will be that. I, myself, shall call. The manager will not be happy at my, ah, stealing his business, but we are friends. Welcome, Lancelot Holliman."

He had one hell of a good grip.

"Come," his wife said, reaching for my hand. She had a good grip, too. "I shall show you the gardens while Luisa rests and finishes her book." She flashed a look at Sable Montanelli's mother, whose name I assumed was Luisa.

"Perhaps Mister Holliman would rather rest, change clothes, bathe," Luisa suggested, without looking at her paperback, "after that long train trip."

"Please call me Lance," I said, feeling myself tugged strongly up out of the strangely comfortable, very yielding wicker chair by the heroically-built Elisabetta Fanfani. "And . . ."

"And he is young, and handsome, and would far rather walk through the garden with a beautiful woman than worry about resting now, eh?" she said. Tugging. She'd got my wrist clamped intimately between her upper arm and the big soft pillow of her left breast, and the warmth there was immoderate, but certainly not unpleasant.

I decided that she was indeed beautiful, nose or no, particularly since she thought so and could say so with such charming ease.

"Si," I said, and got myself led off into the gardens by that big beautiful woman of about forty-five or so, with a body like a collection of pillows. Shaped pillows, I hasten to add. Elisabetta wasn't *fat;* big everywhere and plump. That's it.

She wasn't exactly what can be called kittenish, because she was better at it than that. But she certainly was seductive, and I wondered about the virility and potency of that big virile-looking man who was her husband.

I shouldn't have!

Luisa Montanelli and I were welcomed, and we were accepted, I realized that night after a sumptuous supper, but we were not treated as guests; that is, the Fanfanis didn't feel responsible for our entertainment. People sort of disappeared after dinner, and I sort of wandered. In the huge library, I couldn't find the light switch, then noticed the double doors, glass, leading out onto a little balcony that overlooked the beautifully-tended grounds behind the big house. I went through the doors and out onto the balcony, enjoying the night air: real air, with the smell of trees and flowers in it, along with the sounds of insects and some sort of birds. The trees sighed gratefully as a gentle breeze stirred them. The sky was so clear that even the attenuated moon cast a pallid light over those lovely grounds.

Then I saw that a show had been scheduled,

though certainly not with me in mind. Two people were out there, on the grass, right beside one of several curlicued lounges of white metal. The two people were only partially dressed. The two people were lying down. They were also closely united and in agitated activity. My brows rose as I realized I was gazing at a pair of lovers.

Little moans rode the night breeze, coming from her throat, and I could hear occasional grunts and the slap-and-slurp sound of flailing bodies. Moving into the darkest corner of the balcony, I leaned on the rail to watch shamelessly. While they screwed shamelessly. Or maybe shamefully. For after awhile I realized that I was watching, not a couple of servants, but Luisa Montanelli. And *il Conti* Girolamo Fanfani!

She was doing her part, I could certainly see that. The big woman was rolling her hips about so as to get every surface of her oozing slit scrubbed by his noble cock. Her legs were thrust wide in total abandon, knees raised, while her hips rotated and her juicy, luscious tits jiggled and joggled liquidly. Each of her sighs was a soft little moan that I heard clearly. Feeling the tug of sensual arousal, I imagined the feel of it; her large belly providing superb padding, while her full sexual interior lunged up and down the old dork, swallowing it again and again. Standing out there on the balcony in the moonlight, I shivered.

The count was doing all right, too. I could see him prop himself up on his palms, drawing his loins back from her, nearly all the way. Then he sent his Florentine flagpole surging back into his iniquitous innamorata. Her waving legs snugged him to her, working to prevent his pulling so far back again, snugging him to her, sweaty and groaning in undiluted passion. I could actually hear the slapping sounds of his hard, furrowing strokes. Now he was increasing the tempo and intensity of his deep drives up her belly, his smallish ass rising and falling, thwacking her crotch with his again and again. Assuming he had some length to his tool, I knew he was driving far up inside the writhing, moaning, whimpering body that jerked beneath him in undeniable pleasure.

Suddenly the thought slid across my mind: *Dammit! I wish her daughter were here!*

I had a horn on up to here, and it was painful. I really hadn't realized that watching and listening to others copulating could be so damned exciting.

Again I watched him prop himself above her on his palms, planted firmly on the grass beside her supine body, so that they were united only at the loins. He poised there, the moonlight pale on his pale butt, watching her watch him nervously and expectantly. An athletic lover. Then she started moving up and down, hard and fast, and I smiled. *Hey, good shot, Count!* I thought in admiration. He thought so, too; he was still, poised above her and imbedded in her, glorying in the pervading ecstasy and plain, good old ego-boosting joy of being screwed by her; by his houseguest—the wife of another man.

"Yum," I muttered, absently taking myself in hand.

And at that instant someone else took me in

hand, someone from behind me, who pushed her big soft pillowy jugs up against me and enwrapped me with both her strong arms. A hand clamped on my swollen crotch.

"Move aside," she whispered, deep-voicedly, "you're blocking the view!"

I swallowed, hard. The voice, the big jugs, the ring-bedecked left hand putting the clamps on my fly—it was Elisabetta Fanfani! The countess! Jockeying with me for position at the balcony rail, to watch her husband balling her houseguest! Suddenly I was helplessly taken by qualms, internal shudders; I had read and heard about the hot-blooded reaction of Italian women to their husbands' philandering!

Still, Elisabetta was, I knew, definitely endowed with only the customary two arms, and both of them were accounted for. So were both hands. One clutched the big swollen yard stretching the front of my pants. The other was slipping some very warm and decidedly devilish fingers into my shirt. Neither held a butcher knife, meat cleaver, gun, or the like. True, one was trying to wrap itself around a vehemently volatile weapon, but there wasn't anything she could do to the *count* with it.

"Ah—you'd better slip back-inside, Countess.
. . ."

"Ha," she whispered, squeezing until I began to fear she might be entertaining thoughts of taking out her vengeance on *my* cock. "Go back inside, with you out here—and this lovely thing in your pants, about to-to-to waste-a? Not likely, *mio*

110

Americano toro! And you are not to call me 'countess,' either!"

"Uh-mmm—but . . ."

"Do you think I do not know, perhaps, who isa out there? Are they not *beautiful?* He is making her a prazzunt of the hospitality of the Fanfani— and she is so grateful! Anda you—the hospitality isa extend itself to male guests asa well!"

"Oh." So that was the story. Official Fanfani hospitality, hmm? Well, I might have turned down big Elisabetta, another time—but not tonight, with those squirming figures out there in the moonlight, and her hand on my hard-on, and those big ballooning boobs of hers trying to crush either themselves or my spine, or both!

"Stepa—back . . ." she urged, tugging, and I stepped back, and back, rubbing my butt against her crotch, and then she was releasing my prong and stepping around past me, in front of me, flashing me a big grin betimes, and then she was at the rail, and planting her hands on it, well apart, and bending forward, turning her short-skirted stern up at me enticingly, a broad and decidedly delicious, volatile voluptuous arse, its halves opulently orbiculate. Swaying a bit, she looked back at me over her shoulder.

"Thisa give you the idea, perhaps?"

It gave me ideas, definitely. I smiled and nodded happily. Tugging down my zipper, I managed to extricate my prodigiously swollen poker from my pants and shorts. With it waving in the breeze before me, I set my hands to her broad hips and caressed their broad-swollen smoothness. Then, as

111

my hands slithered upward, they tugged her skirt with them. It slithered easily along her smooth skin. First I saw the tops of her stockings, dark against the swollen ridges of very pale skin they forced to bulge out above them. Then the beginning lower moons of her big buns, and then that tight crack—and my eyebrows ascended my forehead as her skirt ascended her ass; she wore no pants!

All the better to facilitate this little scene, I mused, wondering if her panties mightn't well be crumpled on the floor just inside the library behind us.

I slid my hand in between her sturdy thigh-tops, meaty and close-pressed and radiating warmth like a pair of self-contained furnaces. Swiftly she got her legs farther apart, incidentally lowering the target. My fingers discovered it, furry and soft, hot and moist, lips parted from birthing a kid or two, and from years of apparently steady and happy amoral plumbing by not only her noble husband, but by various houseguests as well. That thought didn't put me off the least; I could have gotten it off that night inside a toothless old prostitute!

A couple of exploratory fingers slipped easily up inside that wet tunnel to her womb, and she shivered and sighed, then wagged her broad pale hips in a provocative little dance that didn't move her feet—but certainly moved me!

"Hurry," she whispered, looking back again and thrusting backward with her upturned beam. "We must try to finish with them!"

"Oh," I murmured, bending both knees and

guiding my swollen lance up under the arch of her wide-parted legs, *"must we? Well then—one tries!"*

And I straightened, planting myself way up inside her in a violent penetration that damned near tipped her over the railing.

That was unwise of me, since it should have elicited a cry of *some* sort from her. But that estimable woman held it back somehow, and then my body was slapping her naked bottom hard and fast as I stroked ceaselessly in and out of the ravenously hungry hole of her vulva. Her capacious quish swallowed my rod and squeezed it, all along the thick stem.

No, I'm not going to say she was young, and tight. But she was experienced, and enthusiastic as only a turned-on older woman can be.

There's an old poem about the felicities of fornicating with more mature women:

They don't yell.

They don't tell,

They don't swell

And they're grateful as hell!

I couldn't think of a rhyme to add then, but suffice it to say that some of them, like the Countess Elizabetta Fanfani, are also enthusiastic and possessed of just marvelous expertise in the necessary movements, internal and ex-.

In the garden, the missionary-positioned count and his guest were busily bringing each other off on the grass, without the alas.

On the balcony, his wife's bowed body was getting all the hot sword of love I could give her, and her head lolled from side to side as she thrust herself back. Badly muffled sounds of pure lust issued from her open, panting mouth. An almost savage fury of wanton delight and need had taken the big woman and she scrubbed the pants I still wore with her shaking, bouncing ass.

I kept pumping, sliding my hands over her, watching the pumping couple in the garden below, feeling the quivers in my straining legs and not giving a damn. I knew she was rapidly approaching her own boiling point, the same as I. She met my hard deep strokes with torrid enthusiasm. Elisabetta was jerking and circling her big juicy bottom wildly, shivering in lustful frenzy while she screwed herself back onto the hard, heavy pole of my dick.

The whole scene was nutty. That was her friend, her houseguest out there, bare ass working away on the slick grass. And that was her husband out there, trying to grind that squirming bottom right down through the grass and into the earth. And behind her, behind Elisabetta that is, was another guest, a man twelve or more years younger than she, and a man she'd just met. Me.

And all four of us happy as larks, lusty as minks, making it like rabbits!

The first squeal came from Mamma Montanelli, and when I heard that keening sound and saw how her legs jerked, I knew she had made it. The big, quivering white legs clamped onto the count's little bottom, and her heels pounded it as he jerked it up and down, pounding her loins. Then I saw him stiffen, and quiver, and jerk, and I knew the fierce-mustachioed old boy was slamming his juice up into her. Gasping and trying to keep from groaning aloud, I moved faster and faster, not anxious to be standing here rearwardly screwing his wife when Fanfani recovered from his throes and prurient preoccupation and began to see and hear again.

Elisabetta concurred in my desire to get off quickly and get out of sight before the other couple discovered us. She strained backwards with her big buttocks, working them against me in a way that made them try to flatten out, bulging to the side— and that forced me deeper and deeper into that straining, humid vagina wrapped around my slick meat.

"Ha—hunnnnnnngh!" she groaned, so that I knew from the sound and her sudden shivers that she was flying over the edge. I adopted the predictable course; I hunched harder and faster, and soon completed my passion's course, too. I may have been last, but I'll bet I enjoyed it no less than the other three outdoor ballers that nutty night!

"Ah—ummmmm," Elisabetta said eloquently, straining hard to clamp down. Then she eased forward, slid her inundated gap off my dying dork with a little plopping sound, and straightened. Her skirt dropped over her big hams. Turning quickly, she flashed me another smile, touched my cheek with her fingers and my mouth with her lips, and hurried back inside.

"God, you're a tiger!" the voice of Luisa Montanelli said, and for a moment I thought she was directing those pretty words at me. Then I remembered that I was invisible—or hopefully—and I backed away, then re-entered the house.

115

I had crossed the darkened library and was in the hallway outside, making ready to drag my tail up the steps on weak legs and collapse on my bed, before I realized that my wilted organ was hanging obscenely out of my fly like a wet pink tongue. Storing it swiftly away, I hurried up the steps, leaning rather heavily on the rail and using it to drag myself along.

But I might as well have left it hanging out. Elisabetta had vanished, doubtless to her own room and her tub or bidet, and the hallways and stairs were deserted. The house was tomb-silent, except for the ticking of the huge clock at the foot of the steps; it sounded impossibly and blatantly loud, in the silence.

The whole damned place is deserted, I mused, but then I entered my room and had to change my mind.

CHAPTER EIGHT

I haven't mentioned the Fanfani offspring because it hasn't been necessary. Until I entered my room that evening, their existence was germane to nothing in this narrative.

There were four (and probably still are). Romano married a little shopgirl from Rome and was promptly, duly disowned—until after a couple of years when he brought her and the kid home. That melted the hearts of Girolamo and Elisabetta, and Romano was re-included in the family. His wife was accepted, too. Elisabetta, junior, was also practically disowned when she decided she wanted to be an actress. But when she made the film "Savonarola" with Federico Farentino directing, and got a couple of nice writeups, she, too, was reinstated into the good graces of her parents. There were some rumors about her and Clint Eastwood, but he returned to the States and a new fame in "Misty" and "Dirty Harry," in both of which he got to wear clean clothes. Sabetta, as she called herself, went off to Germany to make "Mozart" and other things. Now the family was proud of her; our daughter the famous actress! I had to pretend I knew all about her, although in truth I'd never heard of her.

The other son, Girolamo junior, was now eighteen and practically imprisoned, being educated by Jesuits. His father the count wanted no more slipups, and wouldn't it be nice if a boy with his intelligence and family backing would become a priest and maybe make it onto the Curia or even the top seat!

Then there was Giulia, Sable's friend, who had entered a convent at seventeen, a little over a year before my arrival at her parents' villa. By now she was close to the final stage of *non-nuptae*-hood. But she hand't been mentioned at dinner, so I didn't bring her up either. I didn't think about it, or about her. *Religueses* I don't understand, and certainly they aren't my cuppa.

It was Giulia who waited in my room when I entered that night, only minutes after making it with her mother down on the balcony.

It's quite a surprise to walk in, close the door and switch on the light, and turn to find a white-robed *nun,* in one's digs! And when one's penis is still fairly dripping from lasciviously lovely pursuits, it's even more of a shock.

118

But there she was, sitting in the chair beside the bed, all swathed in white. The only visible portions of her were her hands, her ugly shoes, and her pretty face, gazing blithely at me as if she belonged there.

Did I say shock? That was as nothing compared with the shocks she then proceeded to hand me, one after another, until I was reeling and wondering if I hadn't left the haunt of Italian vampires to enter that of lunatics. Lecherous lunatics.

She stood up, still gazing at me from very dark eyes. She was not tall, little over five feet. My perennial wonder about what nuns did with their hair was soon solved; she divested herself of that silly, ugly bonnet to reveal the tight white band that vertically encircled her head, then got rid of that, too. Hers was a short cropped, shining cap of flossy black hair, raggedly banged and arranged in long curling sideburns that looped up onto her cheekbones. Very pretty. Some might have wondered about the possibility of her being a lesbian, to have seen a young woman with such short hair, but I try not to think in bigoted clichés.

"Hello," I said, more uncomfortable than somewhat.

"Buona sera," she said in a very soft voice, like butter sliding over little bells, and she removed her shawl. Then, while I stared, off came the hard shiny white thing that looks like shirt-cardboard and forms a carcanet for nuns, covering the bosom and jutting outward to disguise any possible jut beneath.

"Ah—sister. . . ."

"Call me Giulia, Lance."

"Ah, Giulia. . . ."

"Just be quiet a moment, Lance, won't you? I feel almost as if I know you. . . . Sable just *did* have to talk about you, you know."

"Oh. But—Sister—Giulia, you can't. . . ."

"Is *my* home. You will please not to tell me what I can and can not do in it. Have you not heard of the Fanfani hospitality?"

"Ah, I, ummm . . ." Poke no fun. It was not a situation conducive to witty or intelligent, or even coherent repartee. The situation: the white-clad nun in my room was continuing to come out of her habit! My mouth sagged and I am sure my eyeballs bulged.

I regret that I cannot answer the ancient burning question: what do nuns wear under their habits. In the first place Giulia wore a novitiate's garb, not the official habit. And in the second place, I doubt very seriously if what she wore beneath was convent G.I. What she wore in the way of undergarments, in point of fact, was what one would call decidedly kinky.

The hose were very black, very shiny, and hip-length, making her legs look far longer than they were. And beautiful. They were held up by four black straps, of about forefinger thickness, that depended from her garter belt. It was skimpy, sexy, and—jaguar print! So were her panties, although since they consisted of a couple of fore-and-aft triangles linked by a spaghetti strap, the phrase is g-string, rather than panties. Giulia's "panties" made modern womanhood's so-called briefs look as

120

dowdy and voluminous as Grandma's big navel-to-thigh cotton panty. They were somethin' else, those panties: *Look! Here's where it's at, man!*

But I didn't just stare at those jaguar-print panties (maybe it was ocelot; I know more about women than other predatory animals). My eyes had to rise to the bra, too. There were the usual cups, and shoulder straps, and around-the-back cinch strap. But without buckles, indicating the stretch-thing was a pullover. Too, it was the same brown and black and tan jungle cat pattern. And besides—"cups" is the wrong word. Try half-cups. The bra was there, all right, but the cups left bare her truly lovely red-brown nipples and areolas, then called attention to them because the shoulder straps were divided into two just below her collarbones. That way they framed the gleaming, drum-taut flesh of her beautiful, springy looking love-gourds.

We stood there and looked at each other. I know her gaze was considerably clamer than mine.

"Whew," she said, giving her lovely body a sinuous little writhe. "Boy, does this beat that damned habit!" She kicked the crumpled white garment on the floor and grinned at me. "There! I've kicked the habit!"

"But—you can't—a *nun* . . ."

"You knew I went away to the convent about a year ago? To be exact, fourteen months ago. To be more exact, fourteen months, two weeks, and one day ago." She lifted her arm to consult her watch, strapped on with a thick leather band. "To be more exact . . ."

121

"That's exact enough," I said, waving a hand and wondering if I were capable of moving my other extremities. One of them was beginning to move itself, despite the fact that it had just achieved a delightful detumescence, no more than fifteen minutes before. To be exact, thirteen minutes and some seconds. . . . "Yes, I knew that."

"Ah, and did you know that I *hated* it, that I stayed a year, and then when they started talking about marrying me to Christ, putting a wedding band on me and a lock on me at the same time— figuratively—nuns don't *really* wear iron pants—I knew I'd had enough. What I wanted wasn't marriage to the Prince of Peace, you see, but to get a few male prints on my piece! So I left." Again her long-looking, black-clad leg swung slightly, and again she kicked the habit.

"No," I murmured, "that I *didn't* know."

"Well," she said, walking slowly toward me, swaying and utterly magnificent and totally sexy, "now you know. And the Fanfani hospitality. Do you know about that?"

I nodded. "I know about that."

"Don't tell me you saw them, too? I've been watching from up here, father and Luisa Montanelli out on the grass—and it made me just frightfully horny, too."

I nodded. "I saw them. I was on the balcony, outside the library."

"And . . ." she was nearly to me now, smiling lazily, swaying her hips with explicit exaggeration.

"It made me just frightfully horny, too."

"Well, then . . ." She stopped. Maybe it was in

my eyes, or the set of my face—or lack of set of those flaccid muscles, shocked into looseness. "Oh, NO! Not—don't tell me—not MOTHER!"

With a sigh I lowered my gaze. And nodded.

"That old BITCH! Boy, she'd better have left something for ME!"

"I . . ."

But then she was there, against me, and her arms were rising slowly, going up to my shoulders, and her barely-covered crotch was moving gently against mine, meaning that she was on tiptoe, for she was not at all a tall girl, despite what those fantastic hose did to and for her superbly shaped legs.

We kissed. My hands went over her back, feeling the sleekness of her warm skin and the slickness of the animal-patterned satin. Her tongue left her mouth to push up against my lips, then inside. I felt her shudders as we kissed, tingling thrills surging through her to make her sigh continuously, vocally, into my mouth. She continued writhing her crotch against me. And her breasts, which were softer than they appeared in that strange almost-bra. Soft and very warm and womanly.

It's a little ridiculous, and a little difficult to admit, but—well, to use an old phrase that is supposed to come from the woman: *I found myself* nearly unclothed before I was really aware of what was happening. And then I was cooperating, and I was *wholly* unclothed. And a lovely, cool young hand was half-wrapped around my half-erection, the soft palm gliding up and down, slowly, slowly up and down—until the half-erection swiftly achieved full status and tried to drive a hole into her little belly. The satin garter belt hurt the so-sensitive glans.

"Oh, isn't that *lovely*. Let me taste it!" she sighed, smiling prettily and letting her hands caress their way down my nakedness as she sank to her knees before me. My balls tightened up like overinflated tires. On trembly-weak legs, I stood there and looked down at her, watching that gleaming cap of short black hair lower itself slowly, titillatingly, to my hard and hard-throbbing penis. I felt her sweet warm breath . . .

"Arrrrrgh!" she practically cried out. "You smell like MOTHER!" Her nails dug into my buttocks. I grunted. Then she was looking up at me, pleading with those great soft, dark eyes. "Won't you please go into the bathroom, into the shower—and then come back to poor needy Giulia?"

Pausing only long enough to bend and raise her to her feet, then brush her lips with mine, I posthasted to the bathroom.

When I emerged, clean of cock and other places as well, the room was dark, my bed was unmade, and the oversheet was pleasantly lumpy over excellently constructed woman. With only her head and one shoulder out of the sheet that covered her, Giulia smiled at me.

"You are going to leave the bathroom light on, aren't you?" she asked quietly.

I nodded without speaking and hurried to the bed. With my penis already starting to ascend again.

"Oh—lovely! I get to get it back up!"

She stretched out a hand to me, at the same time

thrusting her head toward my soft-on. The rounded shaping of her pretty mouth was pregnant with indubitable signification. I moved swiftly closer to hand and mouth. The hand went to my hip, cool fingers on my butt. The mouth came down to my dong, and it was not cool. As she stretched a bit, the sheet slipped down off her shoulder and I saw that she had gotten rid of the half-bra, and that her breasts looked just as firm and pretty without its dubious support. Pretty things, lovely sculptured roundnesses that were quite satisfyingly fabulous without any sort of exaggerated descriptions. Nice, pert little dark pink noses set in darker rings, with a touch of brown in their appealing pigmentation.

She parted her sweet lips slightly, then opened wide. She didn't bother with preliminary licking, but nibbled, rather daintily, teasing the rounded head of my cock, which, at half-mast, began pulsing immediately higher. Enthralled and enthrilled with what she was doing, I tried to will the damned thing to take it easy, stay soft, and enjoy the ride. But then her mouth slipped over the head, all of it, and I groaned as she immediately began pumping me with her warm mouth, drawing it in and out, over and over. Her mouth was a hot, wet suction pump that pulled strongly at my yard until my eyes started to glaze. I stared down at the sweet-mouthed, defrocked almost-nun in a trancelike state of sensual stimulation.

"Oh lord," I gasped out, "oh lord, you're beautiful! That's beautiful!" I didn't move. But my hips did, and my penis did. The hips surged back and forth in gentle movements; the thickening staff surged up and up until it was a broad, red-skinned ramrod stabbing into her face.

She rolled her eyes up to meet mine, then grinned with absolutely beautiful lewdness around the pink pole impaling her face. There was a lot of that pole; she was breathing through her nose, now. Her nostrils flared wide with each exhalation.

"IIIIIII-I think you'd—better—just ease off on that—now," I gasped.

Repeating that salacious grin, she gave it a good long suctioning pull, then slid her mouth back and off the nicely glistening shank. I bent, sliding my hands in to palm each of her breasts from the side, and pressed a long, warm kiss on the lovely, lip-stickless mouth that had just done such nice things to my penis. This time it was my tongue that slipped into her face, and she sucked it in response to the new, softer impalement of her mouth. Her breathing stepped up. She began to move, wriggling, pressing her soft tits into my hands. Our lengthening kiss seemed to flog her passions, to fire every nerve of her squirming body.

"Ummmm," she sighed into my mouth. "There's just—no *urgency* about you, is there? You *are* a lover!"

The stress she laid on the word "are" reminded me that I was being not only laid but tested. Sable had dropped some words on this lapsed novitiate about me. I was in that sticky position: coming on with a reputation to preserve and enhance. I tried to get that out of my mind. Everything is better when you just *do it,* let it happen, flow along, without thinking of where you're going, of reputation or orgasms of whatever the *ultimate* goal is. Each moment represents a new goal, instantly giving way to another. Things needn't *lead* anywhere; things can, and in my mind, should be enjoyed for themselves. If there's a long-term goal, such as finishing the chapter you're reading or finishing the book, or the game you're playing, or winning that game, or—getting laid, or reaching orgasm: whatever; fine then, enjoy the moving toward it. Surely only alcoholics and people in a hell of a hurry think in terms of *finishing* a drink. The rest of us enjoy the experience of drinking, and each sip is a new goal. Which may be sententious or something like that, and I'd better return to the loving of Giulia and Lance.

What I did was get involved with her body, pressing and then kissing her pretty breasts, then the shining area between them, and down onto her practically nonexistent belly, still garter-belted, and then farther down, to the beginning swell, the nascent bulge of her pubis and its rich coating of shining black fur. She moaned softly, sighed, and fell back. Her black-stockinged legs opened more and more. The small amount of pale flesh revealed and framed beneath the garter belt, the small amount of thigh flowing almost whitely up out of the black stockings; these formed a pale frame all around the raven-haired luxury of her vulva. There I now set my mouth and tongue, brushing it back and forth over the dark soft fur, slicking it, pressing it down as if pomaded, plastering it more and more to her

127

until it more definitely outlined the upward thrusting shape of her prominent love mound.

Then I found the springy lips, and clamped my mouth with firmness over them. I added a fervid suction, along with a thorough lingual swabbing, until she groaned loudly and clamped, imprisoning my face between her nyloned thighs; flesh, too, soft as nylon. I had found the firm little trigger with my tongue, but had hardly touched it. I liked the feel of her sex, the aroma of her sex, and I waited until she relaxed her leg's grip on my head. Then I slipped my tongue out again to twiddle her pulsing button. Her vaginal trough welled up wetly—and her legs clamped again. She clung, squeezing my head between her surprisingly strong, savory thighs with a relentless pressure. Again I used my tongue in that welling slit, having to part the firm and close-pressed lips, and again I let her feel sharp, stiffened tongue on her pulsing clitoris.

And again she tightened. And that is the way we proceeded, with her tightening up and squeezing, almost in agony in reaction to the onslaught she craved so desperately but could hardly bear.

With mouth and tongue I massaged that little vulvar nipple and caressed the moist lips soothingly until they became more and more moist, both from within and without. Then she was making noises from the throat, noises that were intense and almost ugly, and her muscles twitched uncontrollably. She stiffened, jerking and arching her body, and that warm woman who had almost become a nun came beautifully, absolutely beautifully—a long, sating, relaxing orgasm that left her soft and weak and sighing, and pulling lovingly at me with soft, slightly quivering hands while smiling gratefully and sighing, and sighing, pulling me up beside her to kiss me with soft, un-urgent warmth.

I was suffering from a severe attack of urgency, and she knew it, and once she had recovered her strength she rose above me.

"Oh, you are beautiful," she said quietly, and her eyes glowed. I suppose mine did, too, as a result of those words and her tone! *"You are choice—now lie there and enjoy!"*

And she sucked me off, and it was both choice and beautiful.

In the morning we at last united our genitals, and she was just as tight as I had found her with my mouth. It was exquisite experience, for both of us. Yet what we felt was as much *gratitude* to each other as anything, and there was no tingle, and by the end of the day I had discovered she was practically incapable of conversation. Yes, we made it again that night, because we both wanted to. But the next day I left them, bidding a glowing Luisa to say hi to Sable for me.

It had all been too perfectly lovely, this time, for me to waste time worrying about the lack of tingle with Giulia (thank God it hadn't been there with her *mother!*). I just sprawled out on that swift train and thought about what had been at the Fanfani villa.

Meanwhile—some venal vagrant on that damned train lifted my little overnight bag. Damn!

It wasn't just the bag, or the brand new bottle of expensive Italian after-shave I had just packed in it. But when I thought of all the trouble I had gone to, getting the damned thing out of the Castel di Stresa and lugging it all the way down to the hotel in Rome . . .!

CHAPTER NINE

"Are you an American noble?"

The question was asked by the young woman in my room at l'Hotel de Mer, on the Cote d'Azur, which is the real name for what we call the French Riviera. I hasten to say that the young woman was in my room to good, honest, and non-carnal purpose; she was my maid. She was also a doll. I had arrived so late at the Hotel of the Sea, and consequently risen so late, that she had to wait to make up my room.

Very kind of me to invite her in to do her job while I was present; I had an ulterior motive. She was a doll. I had developed an interest in the interesting development of her body. One of those cute little affairs, constructed economically and with no apparent spare parts or extraneous trim. I watched it move with the suppleness of a working girl, while she straightened up my room. And now she asked me if I were an American noble!

I laughed, sitting comfortably in the room's big easy chair.

"We do not have nobles in America, *cherie*. Just commoners. Matter of fact, recently we've had a spate of the commonest leaders on the planet."

She gazed at me across the bed she was making. One of those unfinished sort of faces, with the infant still apparent in it. Small unturned nose, somehow connected to the upper lip so that its tip rose in the middle. Cute, more than pretty. Fluffy-looking blonde hair, almost yellow. A rounded forehead; convex, shining. Marvelous dimples. And large blue eyes, right now looking a bit distressed.

"Ah—I am so stupeed! Go to the Riviera, darling, my papa said, and perhaps you can rub off some of the provincialism on rich Americans. You are reech Americain?"

Of course she didn't say "the," ever; she said "se" instead, because the French don't pronounce that oddball "th" sound of ours.

"Um," I said, noting the way her effervescent chest tried to bubble out of her uniform when she bent to straighten a little crease in the counterpane. "Oh yes. We all are."

She sighed. *"Oui.* So I 'ave 'eard. And what do you own?"

"IBM," I advised her blithely. After all, Dad has a few hundred shares, and I own an even hundred;

twenty-first birthday present. So we do, after all, own a *part* of IBM. Half a truth's better than none.

"Ummm-m-mmm! That ees . . . exciteeng!" She straightened, running her hands up and down her black, old fashioned maid's uniform. That looked like fun.

I smiled. "Getting excitinger by the minute!" I thought it was cute the way that silly little white doily of a lace-edged apron just covered the crucial area between her hips. Over the black skirt, of course. "What's your name, *provencale?*"

"Vivienne," she told me in her pleasant, rather high voice. "Vivienne Pucher. I am called 'Vivi,' an' I am 'ere two weeks now. From Balles-en-feu."

"From *where?*"

"You see? No one 'ave 'eard of eet!"

I gave my head a half-nod, with a little eyebrow movement. "Uh, it does sound like just the right place for me, right now," I admitted. "Vivi! I like that. And what would you do if I *were* an American nobleman, Vivi Pucher from Balles-on-fire?"

She half closed her pretty eyes and smiled. "Anyseeng. One knows one's place, and se importance of se nobility."

I wondered if she'd ever heard of the Fourteenth of July. But this nobility hangup is—well, common the world over. So are a lot of the nobles.

"Hmmm," I said, then suddenly smiled as a lightbulb snapped on just above my head. "Oh, sorry—my name is Lancelot Holliman."

"Launcelot Holy-man! *Launcelot?*"

I nodded. *"Oui.* Direct descendant," I said, in danger of bolts of lightning from on high, "of the

133

world-be-loved Sieur Launcelot du Lac, of the court of Arthur."

"Oooooh!" Vivienne squealed, and her blue eyes were even wider and rounder. They even looked bluer.

"That makes me almost a nobleman, doesn't it?" I sallied. "I'd forgotten. I mean, *if* America *had* noblemen, of course."

"Oui," she said, almost whispering. Staring at me. Reverence, was that it? close to it.

"You are beautiful, Vivi. Such beautiful legs— are they as beautiful all the way up?"

She looked down. "Aren't seese long skirts atrocious? And seese *awful* black hose! Like a nun! You are too kind, I am sinking."

"I'm rising—oh, thinking," I said, also thinking: about the last nun I'd met. "Well, the stockings don't go all the way up, do they?"

She giggled, dimpling just beautifully. "Of course not!"

I smiled and leaned back in the chair, giving her a steady gaze. Encouragement, expectation, not challenge. She succumbed to the temptation and the silent invitation to display the rest of her pleasantly calfy legs.

Up came the long, black maid-skirt. Revealed were the red-gartered tops of the severe black hose, along with startlingly white thigh-tops. The garters were tight, but her thighs were so firm-fleshed and well-packed that there was no fieshy bulge of bloodless flesh. But that was all secondary in the startling category.

Like, Vivi wasn't wearing any pants.

134

Or slip.

Far more interesting than her thighs was the palecurled forest of Venerian delight she displayed. It twined sparsely over the full fat bulge of her pubic hillock, and her slim, taut thighs made the bulge seem even more prominent; almost a violent thrust.

She seemed quite casually unaware of her lack and of her display, nor did the fact that my eyeballs and crotch snapped to attention appear to have any tendency toward putting her off.

"Beau!" I observed profoundly. *"Tres beau!* Vivi—come a little closer, *s'il vous plait."*

She *plaited;* she came a little closer, not embarrassed but not quite smiling, either. Happy. I kept my eyes where they'd been, though, not on her face. Now I could see the pink seam running up the center of her curly, tendrilly bush. Tight-looking little thing. Looked like a dangerous place to get into. A tight spot. Possible trap. But then, one thing I have never been accused of in such matters is cowardice. In such situations, discretion is *not* the way to get the better part of virtue.

"A—little closer," I urged quietly, leaning forward with more haste than grace.

She still showed no inclination to decline. She advanced with promising promptitude, the black standard of her skirt raised on high.

Now that that pretty little vulva-bulge was just inches from my face, I closed the distance. Bending swiftly forward, I bestowed a kiss on her lightly-furred box—and she came apart, on the instant.

"Ooooh!" she cried softly, almost a little wail,

135

and she jerked violently. A long shudder ran though her and her legs quivered as if they were made of rubber. Oh—oh *Launcelot!*

"Vivi," I said, the word and voice muffled, for I was pressing my face firmly between her thighs, pressing a long, hard kiss onto her brazen bulge. Inhaling, slowly and carefully, without extending my tongue to the delectable dainty; one must first make sure that what one intends to soul-kiss is as clean as one's mouth.

She smelled lovely. I let my tongue slide forth and pass over the silken hairs curling so gently over her mound.

"Gaahh!" she gasped throatily. "Ah, *that* ees a Franch kees!" Her hands slid into my hair, and she tugged gently. Her legs still quivered. She was pushing forward at the crotch, eagerly thrusting her full mound and its little pink pocket at my eagerly thrusting tongue. Her hips wriggled and squirmed in sensuous delight. With her scarcity of pubic hair, and with the extreme softness and delicacy of what little of it was there, it was swiftly easy for me to probe between close-set pink lips with my tongue's tip. I pushed it back and forth just inside her, in her vaginal vestibule, wiggling it at the tip, as I mouthed her precious quish and tickled her thighs with my mustache.

"Ah," she kept saying, in time with her little forward hunches against my face, tongue balling herself, "ah, ah, ah, ah, ah. . . ."

I had moved my hands up to her thighs, then around to her small but very round buttocks, which were emphatically taut, almost hard, so tightly was she squeezing them to thrust her delighted pubis at my face. Holding her firmly, I let the twitching surface of my tongue sink deep inside her.

She, meanwhile, was busily melting. I knew she was melting; I could taste the slippery leakage from her soft inner walls as they melted, as if I were drinking at a warm, sweet fountain. She writhed and squirmed and clutched my hair, forgetting herself and hurting it a little with her tugging, while she moaned at the feeling of my mouth and warm breath and my tongue, a live thing that now speared and lapped inside her. The close-pressed pink darkened, swelled, and drifted more and more apart in response to the warm wet tongue that was squirming over and between them.

"L-Laun—Launcelot—you must . . . Ah, ah, ahhh! You must . . . Please . . . Please take me, take me. . . ."

It had been a long time since I had heard anyone put it in those words, which are by now as old-fashioned as the Victorian "have me." But I certainly wasn't of a mind to chastise her, or chuckle. She had let me know where she was at, very definitely, and responded to everything I said or did, by obedience. She had raised the skirt; she had come closer and closer; and her body had been just as obedient, rising into an instant heat when I pressed my face to its center. She meant what she said; not "let's do it" or "let's share sex" or even "do me." She meant she wanted me to take her.

I rose, letting my hand trail up her leg and cup the bulging area I had left so wet—with a good deal of help from her inner spring. She groaned and ground herself on that hand, at the same time practically tearing open the button front of her dress. She was just beside the bed, not quite turned backward to it, and I started pressing her that way.

For the first time, an expression other than pleasure crossed her face. Her pale brows started descending, and I hesitated, giving her a questioning look.

She glanced back, holding onto her unbuttoned bodice with one hand and my waist with the other. "The—the bed. . . . Could we just. . . . I mean, I 'ave just made it up. . . . I—I *hate* to have to do it again!"

I had to laugh aloud, slipping a finger up inside her as I did.

"One makes so *many* beds each day!" she insisted defensively, and I nodded and laughed the more. And tickled her innards.

Her eyes rolled up and her mouth sagged and her knees lost their stiffness. "S-still," she gasped out, "eef—eef you prefer—then—I weel make eet up again. . . . Just. . . . Oh just take me, feel me!"

I *was* feeling her, but then I realized it was the accent again, that French "i" that always possessed our long "e" sound. She hadn't said *feel* me; she'd expressed a desire to be *filled*. The strain I felt against the front of my pants assured me that I had not only the willingness but the equipment to do it, too.

But I didn't make her make that bed again, after I made her. Instead, I kept my left hand where it was, in her loins with one finger out of sight in a

138

veritable furnace, and I cupped the other beneath one of those taut round asscheeks. Her crotch got a lot of pressure as I lifted her, and she squealed. Then I plopped her little white bottom on the little white table my room boasted, an *escritoire,* and I hurriedly got my pants open and my best parts out where the action was.

With the absolute greatest of ease, I plugged swiftly into her, standing before her while she sat on the shaky little writing table. I felt every micro-inch of that entry, because she was tight and supple. Too, there was the tightening, womb-shaping effect of her being seated on the hard surface. Easily, I anchored my flesh in hers with a thrust that utterly buried me within her humid fissure.

Her eyes went wide and her mouth dropped agape, fighting for breath, then she let out a gurgling cry and seizing me with both hands, ground herself swiftly and forcefully on the big wedge I had driven into her. And, like that, in seconds, she came. Her cry was barely audible, so strongly did she make it, before she sagged weakly against me. Her black-brassiered breasts puched into my lower chest as she lay weakly forward, remaining seated on the table only because I was there as a prop. I knew that if I were to step back, she'd keep sagging forward. She'd most probably have impaled her-self to the trachea, then tumbled onto the floor.

I stood there and held her, remaining well up in-side her. I felt every inner contraction, and they felt just damned good.

Then she came alive. She clutched me, straightened up, grinned in a way that reminded me of the morning sun, and began trying her best to agitate her entire seated body. The pretty white flesh of her tit-tops did its best to escape the deep-cut bra.

"Easy," I groaned, "let me do the moving now. . . ." And I did.

She had come, and she was wet inside. The wet squelching sounds of my big plunger poling almost violently in and out of her sounded sexy, and honestly beautiful, and filled me with both excitement and what must be described as flaming lust. I know I've just gotten through indicating that I'm not goal-oriented. But—so what? There are no absolutes, after all!

So I was goal-oriented. I wanted to blow up inside her, and I stood and hung onto her, and lunged and pulled and pushed until I did. It was marvelous, and damned if I didn't stagger back, exhausted in that post-orgasmic ennui, and—fall onto the bed.

Vivi didn't even look stricken. She just looked delighted and hopped off the table to join me, kissing me with vehement force, again and again.

"Does anyone come around to inspect the beds after you've made them?" I asked after a while, cuddling her close. Both of us were still fully clothed, which was an added fun-thing.

She giggled. *"Non!* of course not!"

"Then we won't worry about the rumpled spread. It's fine. I'll come in tonight and see it, remember, and just grin."

"You are a darleeng!" she enthused, and she kissed me again. Then she pounced up off the bed, collected the tools of her trade, and hurried her seminally-flooded and pantyless little quim out of my room. Probably occurred to her that her maid's cart had been sitting out there beside my door for a long time. And though no one checked, surely there was a housekeeper on the premises somewhere.

Try to imagine that conversation! "What were you doing in nine-bee so long Vivienne?"

"Sitting on the escritoire, madame, being balled by an American nobleman, Sir Launcelot, who left a *lac inside me!*"

"Oh."

Sure.

Chuckling at that thought, I got myself off the bed and went into the bathroom to towel off my penis before returning it to its nest in my shorts. I zipped up as I emerged—and stopped, staring at the table on which she'd sat. I had forgotten about the postcards I had been scribbling away on when Vivienne had knocked and entered! I had used the pen provided, which was not a ballpoint. Now I saw that all the cards had been not only nicely blotted, but smeared, here and there. Penned words feathered with skin-tracks.

I grinned anew. This time I had a mental vision of Vivi's pretty little tail, looking like the Rosetta Stone, with backward English scrawl all over the firm French curves!

But then I sighed and tightened up my mouth. Right. No tingle.

Screw it, I thought angrily, and checked my watch before doing a little mental and international arithmetic. Then I put through the call home. Dad and Mindy were supposed to be back today, and it was not the middle of the night, though pretty late.

He was there; he was fine; he answered himself. Everybody was OK. How was I? Great. Getting any, son? Yep, hahah; what's the news? Well—oh, Cousin Helena, remember her? Yeah, I rememberd her. What about her? As if I cared. Well, Dad advised, Cousin Helena had shaken everyone by running away and getting married—some nasty, arrogant young man from the lower classes. . . .

So *what,* I thought. But I said, "Well, keep your pecker up, Dad."

"Are you serious?" his voice came back, transatlantically. "The poor thing hasn't been up a total of thirty minutes since the wedding."

"Dad!" That's *terrible!"*

"No, it isn't" my father laughed. "It's just that as soon as it comes up, your stepmother tucks it in here or there and runs it right down again."

I chuckled; I'd been worried there for a moment. I knew there was no way he could keep Mindy, or his sanity, without a working tool. And he might *still* have trouble with his sanity!

"Oh, well, super, Dad! Makes you tingle, does she?"

"Extraordinary you should mention that, son. She does indeed, like no woman since your mother—damn her virulent soul."

"Great," I said, dry of throat and fluttery of stomach. "Well, that's about it, I guess. Just wanted to say hi—see you, ah sometime."

"No rush son. Have a ball. Have a *lot* of balls!"

Laughing, we hung up. And my face sobered, quick as a busted neon sign. *Made him tingle, did she?* I sighed and sat back, staring at the telephone, thinking that it sure would be pretty easy to join the rest of the western world and hate the old man!

Then I went down and ate and wandered a bit, finally getting my trunks and oil and meandering down onto the beach among all the bodies. I swam. I sunned. I looked, and I ogled a little. Thinking. All those happy-looking, happy-acting people. How many of them were happy? How many were pretending? How many of those svelte, tanned female bodies wished they had the guts to break off with the moneyed bellies they were attached to, turning themselves into courtesans, which is a nicer word than whores or even mistresses? And how many of them had the brains even to think about it? And . . . how many others hereabouts were on a Quest, as I was? Looking. Seeking. Seeking, and not finding?

I got hot, and gathered up my gear and trekked back to the hotel. There I showered, trimmed a few wild hairs off my mustache, and got dressed for dinner and a night of fun, or something like that.

After having eaten, I just couldn't get my heart into the rest of it; I wound up back in the room at ten PM, which is scandalous. Then I found out that I was just plain tired. I crashed.

CHAPTER TEN

Next day I awoke with the wild idea. I actually rushed through shaving and getting dressed, thinking about it, and very nearly cut my throat when I laughed aloud. Even the European-plan breakfast tasted pretty good; the coffee was warm and the rolls were both warm and fresh. With a smile on my face I sallied forth to brace the world.

Soon I was complicating the life of a salesclerk at the biggest shop in town. She was a most decorative young redhead, and probably thought I was flirting when I told her what I wanted. I probably was. Call it instinct.

I asked for one of evey type and color of Size S panty in the store. She blinked, gazing at me. I watched her slip from the security of her own knowledge of her attractiveness into a state of nervous perturbation. Not to mention incredulity.

"Mi-might one ask—pardon, M'sieu—but why *so many* undergarments?"

I smiled at her, and shrugged. "Panties, panties, not undergarments. As to why so many—hell, the poor dear girl hasn't any!"

Another blink of dark-lashed green eyes. "None?"

I shook my head with unequivocal vehemence. "Not a pair to her name," I assured my clerk across the glass-topped case. "Runs around bare-assed all the time. It's a crime. Think about the winter!"

She shivered. "Think about sitting on cold theatre seats. . . ."

"Leather Mercedes seats!" I offered dolorously.

"Sudden upward gusts of wind!" Again she shivered, but then she seemed to emerge from her little trance; our litany was at an end, with me all ready to fling another into the breach. Breeches. Britches.

"M'sieu, I am . . . Are you serioooos? You really want one of *every* style in se shop?"

I nodded. "Absolutely. The whole shop. In every available color. Panties. Size S."

"Size S."

"S yes."

She sparkled. "M'sieu is too kind!" she said brightly, gazing upon me with the mien of a little girl about to hustle Santa Claus. "Does M'sieu buy so many undergarments for every woman he discovers who possesses none?"

145

"No-no," I assured her. " Only when they are extraordinarily attractive and deserve all the panties they can get."

Regarding me with disarmingly ingenuous eyes, she asked quietly, "And—does M'sieu find me—attractive? As attractive, per'aps, as—as one finds M'sieu?"

"I do indeed," I said, with as much veracity as gallic gallantry. She was, in briefest truth, a damned doll, and the little fisherwoman damwell knew it, too.

Whereupon she glanced swiftly about, fixed me with her green eyes, stepped back a couple of paces, and hoisted her skirt.

No pants. Beautiful patch of red at the base of her startlingly white belly, not a triangular pubic patch, but one of those straight line affairs, running vertically up her mound.

"Hmmm," I said, with what I think can be called admirable resourcefulness, under the circumstances. After all, how often does a *man* get himself accosted by a female flasher? And without even the traditional long coat with nothing under!

"Hmmm," I repeated distractedly. "Perhaps . . . Perhaps we should, ah, repair to a dressing room or the like, and—talk about the styles available."

"Mais oui," she said, letting fall her skirt and flashing me a smile, this time from her *upper* mouth. Then she turned and hurried along behind the counter and into a little mirrored doorway, not without a quick backward glance.

I followed, but stopped short, just around the

146

corner. There was a dainty little pair of passion-pink panties, crumpled where she'd stood. Carefully, hastily, sneakily discarded, and quite expertly, too. I mused, not without admiration.

Soon I was entering the cramped dressing room where the recherché rehead waited, smiling, frankly and unblushingly immoral.

I drew her to me for a lovely, tonguey kiss, during which she was assiduous at teasing my shirt front with the contents of the little bra-cups beneath her blouse. Without a word I removed first my trousers and then my shorts, whilst she stood by with a smallish frown, wondering doubtless at my not having begun with her divestiture.

"Uh . . ." she began, but I smiled and shook my head, and she lasped into silence, presumably with visions of sugarplums and eighty-eight pairs of spanking new panties dancing through her mind. (Is it wicked to apply the phrase "spanking new," to panties?) She continued to regard with high interest my activities—and with even higher interest what I did next: after removing my shorts, I drew my pants back on, tucked in, zipped, and belted.

Then I withdrew her panties from my jacket pocket and showed them to her. She sighed morbidly, her eyes resting unenthusiastically on the evidence of her greed and vagrant ethics.

I nearly wavered in my resolve, then, for she blushed. But for all I knew, she could suffuse her face on cue just as she could strip off her briefs while standing behind a counter no more than a foot from me, without my knowing. Both a physical and ethical gymnast, that one!

I vouchsafed her a stolidly small smile, which she returned with even less enthusiasm, looking chastened, contrite, and nervous. After that I tucked her panties back into the pocket of my jacket and handed her my shorts. She took them automatically, staring at my face.

"Try those, Mademoiselle," I suggested, and departed, leaving her holding, not the bag, but my skivvies. And looking *tres desolee*.

You just turned down a tupping session that would doubtless have been pleasant indeed, Lance me boy, I mused, *and possibly an extended liaison that might have been more pleasant still! Think maybe you're getting a mite old?*

Nope, I advised myself without intimidation or rancor, definitely not that. Just—selective. And about time! Besides, I'm a bit young to be looked upon as a sugar-daddy. Or a panty-daddy!

I accordingly sashayed on down the street and entered another sizable shop. There I deliberately turned an unpleasant mien on an attractive young female clerk, making my way, instead, past her to obtain the services of a plump woman of about fifty, with a face like a used marshmallow.

She was a bit surprised at my request, but nodded, suppressing a charming little giggle. And she fulfilled my order, not without attracting the attention of several others in the shop.

"Your pardon, Monsieur," a portly man with a Pompidou nose and well-brushed gray hair intoned, "but—might one ask . . . Ah . . ."

I favored him with a level gaze and no sign of a smile. *"Oui, M'sieu? Quel est votre probleme?"*

"Ah—ummm . . . That is quite the largest number of, ah, that is, *underwear* that one has ever seen purchased all at, ah, once."

I still gave him no help, but continued to skewer him with an unsmiling, level gaze. It's bastardly, to make people so uncomfortable—but then, nosy people really shouldn't count. I felt *pleasantly* bastardly.

"M'sieu has, ah . . . Well, is that one must congratulate the young monsieur on the number of his—acquaintances."

"Oh," I said, at last breaking into a smile, as if I just hadn't been able to understand what had brought him over, "I see, I see. One thanks you, sir, but one has to admit—there is but one *acquaintance*. Charming old fellow, really, and you'd never know it to look at him, but—well, he has only this one harmless little peccadillo. I suppose we are all entitled to one. *Et vous, Monsieur?* Is it that you, too, have an *interest* in the feminine intimate clothing?"

He became a foot taller, gruffed out "Positively not!" and departed with alacrity.

I wended my bastardly way out of the shop, smiling.

A taxicab was required to transport me and my purchases back to the hotel. The clerk looked up as I entered, giving me that predictable unctuous smile.

"Ah, M'sieu has been *shopping!*"

I glanced furtively around and hugged my vast burden to me. "Shop," I said, lowering my voice

149

and rolling my eyes, *"-lifting!"* And I went up to my room.

Which, I learned very swiftly, an appalling pall descending over my *joie de vivre,* had been searched! Not just searched; ransacked. Place looked as if it had been disported in by a menagerie of malicious monkeys. Clothing strewn about. Bed unmade (poor Vivi!). Drawers hanging obscenely open, contents dragging the floor.

I parked my packages in and around the big chair in the corner and swiftly called the manager, which required seven minutes, as I had to go through no less than three chamberlains. He arrived on the scene all ready to bluster and assure me that I was out of my skull, but the moment he entered that bedraggled room, his eyebrows sought his hairline and he grew visibly smaller. While we were attempting to discuss the situation, the housekeeper appeared, a short and very thin Italian woman with worse French than mine. Soon Vivi, wide-eyed and frightened, was also called upon the scene, and she assured us that she had made the room only a little over an hour ago. She kept shooting glances at me and at all those packages. I suggested that we call the police; the manager begged me to eschew that unpleasant and publicity-attracting course, and made several fine offers in its stead. All three of them then helped me search and set the place to rights.

As well as I was able to ascertain—and remember—absolutely nothing was missing.

At last I grew tired of assuring them that I could think of no reason for this, that I was most certainly not a smuggler or a character out of a Helen MacInnes novel. I ceased talking. They went on awhile longer before they realized I was no longer a participant in the animated conversation. Six eyes swung curiously my way; three mouths closed.

"I find nothing missing, and I know that you are as unable to account for this as I am," I told them, although addressing myself directly to the manager. "I won't calll *les gendarmes,* then, and I shall avail myself of your most kind offer to provide the room without charge. And now I would wend my way backward, and please pardon me, but would you leave my room to me?"

Mention was made of the rumpled bed—by the housekeeper, not Vivi—and I advised that it was fine. Eventually they departed, and I sat down quietly to have a little talk with myself.

It came to nothing. I couldn't think of any reason for anyone's searching my hotel room—or merely being mean by wrecking it, either.

Obviously, I thought, heading down to the beach, *this is my lucky year with women—and not otherwise. First I really mucked up my overnight bag, dropping it out of the Stresa castle. Then someone ripped it off. Now someone's tried to rip-off my room. Well, I guess as long as the good fortune with females continues, and as long as no one tries to rip ME off, I shouldn't complain. I'll just. . . .*

I stopped short. The slim blonde who stood there staring curiously and a bit nervously at me was not only very lovely indeed, she wore the teeniest bikini bottom I'd ever seen. Looked like a yellow cocktail napkin, equipped with two shoe-strings that dug slightly and pleasantly into her hips.

"Are you all right?" she asked, with an apparently genuine concern.

I blinked my lack of comprehension.

"You were walking directly toward me, on a collision course," she explained, "and I just kept on coming. I thought you were doing eet deliberately, and I was sure you'd stop. Then as you came closer, I saw that your eyes were fixed, as eef you 'ad been 'ypnotized—and you were—muttering?"

"I'm sorry," I said, blinking. "I guess I was, at that. I've just had a fantastic experience, back at the hotel. Someone broke into my room."

"Oh how awful? And took your . . ."

I shrugged and shook my head. "And took nothing, apparently. But it was a shock just the same. So I was walking along thinking about it, you know, wondering who and why, and . . . Well, I guess I *did* look pretty weird. I'm sorry I, ah, so rudely passed my shock on to you." Then, wanting to get off the defensive as quickly as possible, I said, "But you have now shocked me, too, Ma'mselle. Have you perhaps been snoozing in the sun?"

"No," she said, giving me a little frown, "I've just come out of the water. See how wet I am? What makes you think I've been asleep?" Her hands rose automatically to her face, as if she expected to find some tactile evidence there, huge bags under her pretty eyes, or something.

I glanced aroud, then leaned forward confiden-

152

tially. She responded as I'd expected, turning her head slightly to one side and also becoming conspiratorial of expression and attitude. "No," I mutteed. "You look marvelous, and your eyes are beautiful, and yes, I see that you are wet. But Ma'mselle—someone has stolen your bikini top!"

She blinked, gazed at me just a moment, and then burst into a full and very natural laugh. Her naked little breasts jiggled prettily, bobbing up and down with exuberantly positive nods.

"You *are* a comic! Did you arrange all this just as a new way to meet a pretty girl!"

It was my turn to blink. Then I nodded with judicial solemnity. "I confess. You're lovely and alone. I'm alone and lonely, and I hoped if I did something original, like pretending to be sunstricken or something, I might get the chance to tell you I'm Lance Holliman from New York and ask who you are." It was a nice lie. Making people feel good is fun. Ask your local pusher.

"Wow, you're still *doing* it. That's about the most original. . . . I'm Odile Chabrol, and I was on my way to get a coffee, or lemonade, or—something?"

"Amazing. So was I."

She laughed, "You were heading toward the water!"

I shrugged. "You know how it is when one's thirsty," I said, and laughing we walked back up the beach to where it ended in a cluster of bright umbrellas, shading tables and chairs and attentive waiters and waitresses.

CHAPTER ELEVEN

"Yes, it is a frightful waste of money," Odile said with laughing face and eyes, "having to buy a *set* when one requires only the bottom!" She rumpled her chin a bit to look down at herself. "But why should one cover one's breasts—particularly when there is so little to cover?"

"You're fishing," I said, "Careful, or I'll bite."

She thought about that a moment, then smiled brightly and leaned back, fixing me with a slightly warmer gaze. A promising gaze, that. "Hm, she said, and raised her second glass of iced coffee to her lips. Her eyes fairly sparkled at me over the top of the glass. I tried to make mine sparkle back.

"And does the American Monsieur 'olliman per'aps know of a young women in need of a bikini

top, size not very big? It is in perfect condition—
nevair worn!"

I was unable to think of anyone. "I'll, ah, certainly let you know if I run across another bare-
topped girl who looks less happy about it than you
do, Odile. By the way, your nipples are perking."

She looked as if she might be about to flush, but
she didn't. "You aren't supposed to comment on
something like that!"

"Why not? I'm hoping I get part of the credit," I
smiled. And swiftly raised my glass to drink. It was
a good idea to leave hanging there while one de-
parts, but I was certainly not interested in depart-
ing. I used the glass, instead.

"Hm," she said again, a pleasant sound coming
from a pleasant and pleasantly arranged face. She
pursed her lips thoughtfully. It was fun, sitting
there flirting with a pretty girl who showed every
sign of being liberated, and as flirtatious and interested as I was.

"It would be interesting to see you in clothes," I
told her, bringing what I sought: the reward of another of her lovely, full-faced smiles. "Please have
dinner with me tonight."

She raised her eyebrows, then sighed rather
sadly. Her hand came across the little round table
to touch mine, then withdrew before I could respond. "I couldn't possibly. I'm here with my sister, you see. My twin sister, Odette. I just think
that—well, it would be just grossly unfair to leave
her alone."

"Let 'er run into her own hypnotized, muttering
men," I muttered.

She laughed, but shook her head.

I spread my hands in a French gesture. Hell, here was the crux I'd been afraid of. Stuck again! But I enjoyed being with her, and decided to go ahead and broaden the invitation, at the risk of spending most of another night alone.   Her eyes and teeth flashed when I extended the dinner invitation to include her sister. "You're staying at *l' Hotel de Mer,* Lance?"

I nodded. "I'll go back now. She was writing some cards, I think. Call us when you come in—we're in—ummm, I don't remember. The desk will tell you."

"I'll certainly ask."

We sat and gazed at each other a few moments longer, smiling like a couple of kids. Happy with ourselves, happy with each other. Then she nodded, pushed her glass slightly away, and rose fluidly to her feet. A slim, very sinuous young woman, golden tan, with hair almost white. Not quite model-thin, but her hipbones were in evidence, the tiny bottom of her suit streching across from one to the other undisturbed by belly, of which she had precisely none. Just a cute little convoluted navel, set in the center of a tanned plain.

I started to rise, but she'd already moved swiftly around the table to place a hand on my shoulder.

"No-no. Just be a while. I'm going to go and get my clothes and talk with Odette. If she doesn't care to have dinner with a strange American, come visit me in the local jail—I shall kill her!

And off she went, with ball-tightening hip-and-butt movement. *Hips and butt by Gruen,* I mused, watching—along with a lot of others. *Precision movement!*

Then I sat back, smiling expansively, aware that a number of those male eyes had now turned enviously upon me.

They were twins, all right. Each of them somehow shared the same face, even the same hair, and its length, and eyes, and . . . clothing. This time they were both fully clothed, and very decoratively, too. Like mirror images. Odette and Odile Chabrol. Odile and Odette. Blonde, slim, quick to smile and to laugh, seemingly unaffectedly. Very effervescent, constantly exchanging looks and saying cute things—and both noisily delighted with my suggestion: that they economize by agreeing that one of them would swim bottomless whilst the other went topless.

We had some lovely clams, some lovely wine, and a fancily-prepared shrimp that was superb. And another bottle of wine. It was all just perfect, and so was the fact that we all three got along—and that *both* of them played the game of knee-to-knee and hand-on-leg with me, under the table.

I asked for three cognacs and the bill, and they availed themselves of the opportunity to visit the ladies', together. Public restrooms, apparently, are as much a togetherness thing for women in France as they are in America. I was glad. Their absence gave me time to recover from the bill I signed; it was enormous. I tried to do some mental arithmetic, switching francs into dollars, but I broke down and wouldn't be seen working it out on paper. Besides, for all I knew there had been another dollar devaluation and my figures were off anyhow.

Then the more interesting figures returned, moving sinuously through the dining room in their yellow and white, short dresses and tall white boots, and once again many more eyes than mine followed their progress. They were a striking pair. I rose for them, and smiled at the comment on my old fashioned courtliness.

Then they both leaned forward and fixed my eyes with their sparkling gray ones, eyebrows up. "The point is, Launcelot 'olliman, can you 'andle bose of us?"

I dragged my own eyebrows back down and leaned back to ease the sudden strain in my fly. "Ah—well, I don't know, to be frank. But I did meet Odile first, after all. I'd thought. . . ."

They both laughed. "AHA! *Mais oui, mais—qui est Odile, et—qui est Odette, eh?*"

I stared at *O*—at the speaker. They'd been to the restroom. They'd returned. They looked just alike. How did I know which was not favoring which chair with her pert bottom? And now the mischievous lovelies put it straight to me; first, could I handle them both, and then which *was* Odile, and which Odette?

I leaned back, defeated. The three of us stared at each other.

"Hmp!" *O*—that is, one of them said, poking out her lower lip.

"Hmp!" her twin echoed, duplicating the pout.

Then they both laughed.

"Well, (somebody) said, "you'd better escort

us to our room now."

I didn't interpret that as meaning that the evening was at an end, and I was right. We left the dining room and went up, and, ah, well, *O* and I exchanged a swift kiss while her sister got the door open. She gestured with a flourish; her twin entered, and immediately I received the same sort of kiss from the girl with the key in her hand. It wasn't a goodnight kiss; she pulled me inside.

They were a bit cautious, but eventually we all understood each other, and I nodded. Yes, I'd love to smoke.

Delighted, they hurried together to fetch their dope, which was in a portable radio with no batteries in it, but an assortment of joints, nicely and neatly rolled. I discarded my jacket and sat tailor-legged on the floor, which is sort of the ritual way to blow grass. Odile joined me, on my left. Or maybe it was Odette. Her tucked up legs hiked her tiny skirt nearly all the way to her hips, providing me with a stupefying vision of the frontward bulge of her shinily-stretched white briefs. Then Odette—or maybe it was Odile—joined us, on my right. We formed a neat little triangle, an ashtray on the carpet in our center. Odette lit up. Or Odile. Let's call her Odette. On my left.

Odile and I waited, almost breathlessly, with that bright-eyed expectant attitude that I think must be universal for people waiting for the leader—usually the roller—to get the twisted end lit properly.

Odette got the doobie going, sucked deep and long, and followed that with a swift, over-noisy suck of air. She passed the mini-cigaret to me, and I got myself a good toke before passing it on to Odile. Odette exhaled as her sister sucked. She was ready for her second toke when the joint came her way. No one was saying anything. I exhaled as Odile inhaled, sucked, and passed. And around again.

That feeling of relaxation began to come over me. Not exactly lassitude, not ennui; it's akin to being drunk on alcohol, really, except that you know you're OK, you can operate, and also when you close your eyes the room stays in place. Approximately. I mean it doesn't spin. But why am I telling this; surely by now everyone's smoked but Reagan, and maybe, just maybe. . . .

"Oh, lis-ten," Odette sighed, passing me the joint again.

"That's *good*." Odile enthused, echoing the sigh and visible relaxing. "I get so—so sort of saggy."

"I get so tactile," I said quietly, my voice sounding a little faraway and the words seeming to emerge slowly, and I passed what people used to call the "reefer." And let my hand drop lightly onto Odile's stockinged leg, once she had the stub in hand. After giving me a little smile, she toked.

"Well, spread that tactilil—tactil*ity* around," Odette said, moving restlessly and patting my leg.

I smiled lazily at her and rubbed her knee with mine. Then I closed my eyes, getting a vision of both women being much farther away and that my arms had lengthened so that I could reach them easily.

I started telling them about Andrew Weil's mindblowing book, *The Natural Mind,* about the business of seeking alternate states of reality—which he says is so normal as to appear innate in mankind. I was aware of my voice, aware of forming each word, aware that they emerged slowly and with great care. I kept forgetting what the next phrase was supposed to be, too, and so I shut up.

Odette had produced a clip, and I toked once using it, but declined next time around; we were down into the roach now, and that last one had burned. Besides, it was good stuff. I was where I wanted to be, which was somewhere else from where I'd been ten or so minutes before. Comfortable, very relaxed, enjoying the quivering sweet smell in the air and the quivering sweet feel of Odile's leg under my hand and Odette's against me, I lay back with my eyes closed.

It would have been nice had we had some music. Moody Blues, Pink Floyd, some of the early Doors' material; those are all very nice when you're stoned. Not high. I don't say high about marijuana (I like Weil's spelling better; he spells it as we pronounce it, with an "h" in the middle). I don't feel high. Not the opposite, either, certainly not *low,* because "feeling low" sounds as if you're ill or at least feeling below par. I get above par sensation with good dope, but that utter relaxation makes it different from any other experience. Alternate reality.

Too, there's the fact that everything *feels* better, and I want to *feel* things, and soon I was on my back with each of my hands moving over my companions. My left stroked and stroked through Odette's soft blonde hair; my right slid over her twin's thigh and up over her pelvis, feeling the prominent hip-bone, sliding over the nonexistent belly. It was she who took my hand and moved it up to the nicely firm little half-ball of her breast. I caressed it, sliding the soft fabric of her dress over it until I felt the wakening of her nipple and its perky upward pushing against the material, against my fingers.

Turning toward me on her side, Odette began unbuttoning my shirt. Soon I was getting off on the sliding of her hand over my chest and stomach. Everything very slow; smoke-slow.

"Wha're you doing, Odile?" Odile, asked, and I realized that she wasn't Odile at all. Oh well.

"He's wearing too many clothes," her sister replied in a detached voice, and I felt a vagrant hand dip in under my belt buckle. Mine was on her thigh, and I let it become vagrant, too, a wanderer that moved up over tight-smooth thigh-flesh and fondled the pubic hillock thrusting out her panties. She sighed. My thumb and first two fingers closed, through the dress, around her twin's nipple. She sighed, too. Odile's hand, thrust deeply and rather uncomfortably into my pants, encountered the head of my twitching prod with its fingertips. And I, too, sighed.   Over the course of what seemed an hour or so, we got ourselves out of our clothing. All three of us were pretty incompetent at that edifying task, but we coped, however slowly. How stupid of people to say that blowing dope leads to sex! It's a lot of bother. But it is very nice, because everything is profoundly *pronounced*. Heightened sensation; the opposite of alcohol. As for us three:

we were into the sex before we smoked. All three of us knew we hadn't come up here to discuss international relations, but to have some.

I had a hard-tipped breast in my mouth, and was tugging away at it while gently mauling its mate with one hand. I was superlatively aware of the superlative treatment my cock was receiving; it, like Odile's nipple, was nicely ensconced in a humid mouth that made gentle love to it.

Swathed utterly in the hazy robes of a good deal of good dope, this and that part of our bodies moved as if possessed of a mind and musculature distinctly apart from the owners. Slowly, matters escalated. With an absolute lack of hurry, of urgency, we involved ourselves with one another's physical selves. The movement and suction of Odette's mouth around my erection strongly affected my tranquility. My hand, two of its fingers slithering about within the enticingly and emphatically wet slit of her vagina, was also strongly affecting hers. She was hunching, riding my hand with her body and clamping her firm thighs on my wrist.

I felt the firming of Odile's nipple against my tongue, the seemingly nervous twitch of that erected button, and she gasped and moaned. By now utterly helpless, adrift in a liquid sea of sensual happiness and desire for more, she surged her bosom into my face. She had a hand in my hair, where it felt good. I teased her a little, letting my teeth nibble on the swaying flesh of her lovely small breast, cherishing it with my lips, drawing at its thick dark tip. The fingers of her other hand crept down over my lower belly and slipped into the hair there; mine and that of her sister's head.

"Odile? Let me have that for a while, OK?"

"Uh," Odile replied, "uh, uh!" Because I was slipping my twinned fingers more rapidly in and out of her oozing center now, running up over her clitoris and then back inside the long channel again.

"Oh, damn, dammit," Odette muttered, sliding down and fastening her mouth on my nipple. Her tongue began working rapidly back and forth.

It was good, erotic. I love it. I've been told that a lot of men don't. I think they just don't admit it, as if being erotically stimulable in the same place as a woman somehow diminishes their fragile manhood. Too bad. Women enjoy sucking on little bumps as much as we do; we were all infants once.

Odette sucked and tongued my nipple and played with my lower belly and, I suppose, her sister's hair. Odile sucked softly at my manhood and tickled my anus with a naughty finger. With one hand I stroked in and out of her wet-silk interior; with the other I pressed and caressed her sister's flank and ribcage and breast, while I sucked and tongued its twin.

Odile became more and more agitated, hunching hard and sighing, and then she was relinquishing her oral hold on my cock and sagging across my thighs while she twitched and sighed out her climax. It would have been nice to have gone into her then, but it was far too much bother, and besides, she had her climax and I was involved with her sister. Who, abruptly, released my nipple and robbed me of hers, moving swiftly back.

She moved her sister out of the way, bestrode me, grinning—I watched through eyes barely slitted open, my vision hazed by dope and by my own lashes—and held my saliva-wet organ up beneath her. I held my breath while she came down on it, agilely and expertly, nabbing and swallowing the bulbous head up inside herself, then taking in the whole long cockshaft, I felt it, felt it—felt every micro-micro-millimeter of insliding flesh caressed and gripped by hers.

She began to move, a beautiful, sensuously writhing vision of nakedness and lust and down-driving lunges.

I felt her inner muscles pressuring and sucking as she twisted and turned on my upstanding tool; watched her hand come rushing down to find her clitoris. My own hands, both of them, seemed to float forward and up to her impudent titties, which I began to mold, palpating the pouting pink crests with agile fingers, tweaking them and pretending to pull callously at them. She caught her breath sharply and speeded her up-and-down movements, as well as the movement of her own hand over her stubby little trigger.

She was, as the more expensive and lamentably badly written books would say—fucking me fast and hot.

It seemed that hours had passed. It seemed that I had maintained an erection forever. It seemed that it was going to last forever. In and out, in and out, with Odette moving up and down, up and down, wagging her hips now to move her body in a circular motion all around my turgid but unhurried penis. Her slim, taut-skinned thighs elevated and lowered her with beautiful rippling ease. I lowered my hands to watch her strong-muscled breasts bounce and flop. Beautiful.

"Your tits are beautiful," I told her.

She didn't answer. She was busy gasping and moaning. Her fingers were moving as rapidly over her pressure-valve as her body was rising up and dropping back onto my loins with little slapping, fleshy noises. I smiled.

"*You're* beautiful," I murmured. "What you're doing is beautiful."

And I heaved upward with a sudden straining of my leg and stomach muscles that shoved my cock far up into her and made her eyes bulge. She rode it avidly as I exerted the hardest effort a man can, in lovemaking, and her lovely orange-sized boobs wobbled furiously as she jerked her slim hips in short, quick undulations.

I saw it grab her, saw the sudden sheen as perspiration popped forth from a hundred-thousand pores, saw her shoulders hunch and her eyes roll upward. Then she was jerking and twitching and groaning as if she were undergoing exquisite torture. She succumbed and came in a squirming groaning twisting release that made her inner vagina clamp around me like an angry mouth.

Then she sagged, and collapsed, slipping sidewise to the floor; there was a liquid pop as her body pulled free of mine and my dick surged upward strongly, abruptly thrust out into the cold.

I lay there and thought about that unfortunate

state of affairs for several seconds—seconds that seemed like hours. Then I pushed myself up to sitting position, swung my eyes about over a carpeted hotel room floor, miscellaneously endowed with highly decorative naked bodies.

Lying on her side, Odette smiled at me and mimicked a little long distance kiss. I closed the distance. She turned onto her back, grasped my prong, and pulled. I slipped in between her thighs and easily into her. Then, because I felt a sudden urgency and seemed to need more friction, I lifted my legs one by one and got hers between them. While that gave her far less of me in her womb, it tightened her up and increased my sensation; the whole barrel of my gun was clasped as it prodded down between her thighs and into her liquid pocket. Each stroke felt as if I were burying myself in her, while in truth, the soft lips forming the mouth of her sex held only the knobby glans in their sexy grasp.

I moved faster and faster, feeding the holocaust surging in my loins. Then it burst, and I groaned and ground down onto her while I emptied myself into her. It seemed to go on for hours, my erection detumescing in erupting spurts, quick thick seminal jets that almost hurt as they blasted out of me.

About a gallon, I remember thinking, and then I very pleasantly went to sleep.

It was absolutely lovely, a truly glorious night. Yes, I had been able to handle them both. Both twins with the *O*-beginning names. And that is *my* story of *O; with O's!*

CHAPTER TWELVE

But . . . *no tingle.*

There wasn't much of a hassle, when I awoke at about four AM, feeling tired and chilly and in desperate need of having to piss, in getting myself tucked into my clothes and back to my room and then tucked into bed.

I had forgotten the sign, and it was Vivi who awoke me in the morning. She was abundantly apologetic, and indicated that she'd be glad to join me in bed in some sort of atonement for her sin of waking me. I checked my watch and decided to go ahead and get up. She departed when I said, suggesting that she come back in an hour. Then I rose and got myself ready to face the world again. Before I left the room, I piled my purchases for her on the bed and attached a note:

"Vivi: *tout pour vous. —Launcelot du Lac.*"

Later, after I'd eaten and indulged myself in a hazy remembrance of last night, I returned—to be grabbed in the corridor by a brightly smiling, squealing Vivi. She kissed me soundly and hung on until I peeled her off. Then, without even bothering to check if there were other guests, maids, or the redoubtable housekeeper in the hall, she backed away and smilingly hoisted her skirt to show me one pair of her new panties. She also, after I had opened the door to my room, gave me a moving demonstration of how readily removable those little powder-blue panties were. I was unfortunately incapable of making practical use of that fact.

I was also a little shook; it seemed to me that I had been watched, in the dining room, and followed when I emerged. By the little man who wasn't there. The one who'd searched my room?

I returned to the beach for a long lazy afternoon of sunning and half-assed swimming, and only smiled when, back in the hotel, I learned that the Mademoiselles Chabrol, Odile and Odette, had checked out.

Good, I mused, going up to my room to do things about getting ready to do things about dinner. They're just as casual as I thought, the darlings! A comfortable and wonderfully sexy night, and then departure without complication or tearful *au 'voir.* Thanks, you darling twins—you're beautiful.

A short while later I was thinking about the

beauty of uncomplicated amours, and just reaching for my jacket to go down to dinner, when I heard the knock at my door. Eyebrows up, I answered it. And my eyebrows climbed higher. Uncomplicated amours? Here stood . . . complications!

This complication was barely over five feet in height. With a gleaming helmet of shining black hair, close-cropped, cut in ragged bangs and with long sideburns that sort of looped up, like sickles, onto her high cheekbones. Dark, dark eyes gazed at me. She looked very lovely, and very fidgety, and not very welcome.

"Giulia!" Wasn't that brilliant?

"Ah, Lance," she purred, in that butter-soft voice, "Lance, my darling!" And she practically lunged against me, wrapping me in her arms and prodding me in the abdomen with her so-firm breasts.

I stood there, trying to decide what to do with my arms and hands while she used hers in emulation of a pair of signally amorous—or signally hungry?—boa constrictors. She smelled marvelous. She looked marvelous, a lot better in the printed silk dress than in her discarded nunnish garb. And she felt good. But—Giulia Fanfani? On the Riviera, from Florence—had she followed me?

That was too much to believe, but that was apparently the case, for she was pressing me back into my room, using her entire body as a fulcrum, and telling me that she loved me, loved me, had to follow, could not let me leave, etc etc etc.

"Ah—Julie—umm gee doll, it ah, ain't gonna

happen," I said, wondering why all the pop songs are about unrequitted lovers and how come no one ever thinks sympathetically of the unrequiter.

But she ignored me. At last letting go and giving me a chance to breathe, she stepped back, fixed me with that dark-eyed gaze—and began to peel. Obviously it was her thing, bracing me in my room and coming out of her clothes. This ex-nun had all the instincts of a professional stripper!

I stepped back, holding up my hands, palms out like a cop. "No, Julie. Stop that. Quit it. Don't *do* that, Julie! No-no—it ain't going to happen, Julie. Look, you just came out of a convent—you need some more experience with males. You don't love me, you just—Giulia! Stop, now! You—Jesus!"

The jaguar-print underwear again. Tips-out bra, garter belt, hip-high hose. No panties.

So I succumbed. I don't recall having made claim anywhere in this tingle-less narrative to being an iron man. If I did, ignore it. Only one portion of the Holliman physique ever takes on any aspects of iron, and it immediately wants to do things about achieving earthworm softness again.

In other words, I succumbed.

Considerably later, we rose from my hyper-rumpled bed, dressed, and at last went down to the dining room. My stomach was rumbling like a train in a tunnel.

After we'd ordered, Giulia discovered that she'd lost her purse. Must have left it in my room. I nodded, unable to hold back a little sigh, and started to get up. She pressed a firm hand on my sleeve.

171

"No-no, darling, you must save your strength," she told me, with a positively wicked grin. "Give me the key—I will get it. It is my stupidity—but how could I think of an old *purse* when I have been lov' by *you?*"

I succumbed again, then sat there wondering what the hell I was going to do about her. And then I was wondering what the hell *she* was doing; she was gone a long time indeed. I was considering going after her when she as last returned, hurrying through the dining room, carrying her purse (which I didn't remember her having before, but then I wasn't able to think much, at the time) and smiling brightly.

After jokingly asking the apostate nun if she had searched my room and gaining another smile and a little giggle, I told her about the way I'd found it yesterday.

"You mean—someone *did* search your room? What did they take?" Her nearly black eyes were large and round.

I shrugged, opening my hands expressively in what I considered a suitably Italianate gesture. "Nothing, that I could find," I said, and talked a bit about the experience, which now seemed rather funny. Except that Giulia seemed shook.

We spent the latter part of our meal discussing the fact that I was *not* going to accompany her to her room, there to spend the night. I was adamant. Assured her that I did not love her and that it would not be fair to her. She assured me that she understood, that she had behaved like a silly girl—I remembered that she wasn't yet twenty, at that—

but that it would be cruel, unnecessarily cruel, not a kindness to force her to sleep alone. She had after all come all this way, she pointed out, and she promised that she would depart on the morrow.

Me, too, I thought. And I succumbed again.

We stopped off at my room for the new Dopp kit I had brought, and as I returned from the bathroom with it, my pushy paramour asked about the "handsome overnight case you had when you were—at our villa." She dropped her eyes sadly as she finished the sentence. My eyes narrowed only a bit. It's amazing how so many people spend so much time acting—and how so many of us see so easily through the amateur histrionics.

"That handsome bag," I told her, glancing around my room, "was stolen, Giulia, on the train from Florence! Can you imagine? A twenty-dollar bag and about fifteen dollars' worth of shaving tackle and so on. I can't—hey!"

She had gone white, and she appeared to be more than unsteady on her feet; she was positively reeling.

I sat her quickly down and poured a little brandy into a water tumbler. I also considered loosening her clothes, but it occured to me that it would be badly done; she was certainly far better at that than I! Then I resumed my glancing around, and I observed a few little things about my room.

I sat down on the side of the bed, facing her when she slumped in the skirted chair, and bent forward.

"Julie."

She continued gazing at the floor. Looking very pale indeed.

"Giulia!"

She dragged her eyes up to meet mine.

"Julie—you're a liar. You did *not* follow me here out of love, or even infatuation. You did not *accidentally* leave your purse up here, either. You wanted an excuse to search my room. And you did, Julie." I waved a hand, taking in my digs. "After the joint was ransacked yesterday, see, I did some James Bond-type things, and—all three of those dresser drawers have been opened since we went down to eat! Now look, doll, I can put two and two together, but I think maybe four isn't the right answer. You'd better clue me in."

She stared at me a moment. Then her lip began to tremble, and her eyes went all misty and started leaking, and she began to weep. Looking at the floor between our feet, she clued me in. She talked about having fallen in love with a guy, while she was still a novitiate. She wanted to run away with him. Her coming out of the convent was bad enough; Giorlamo and Elisabetta Fanfani would never allow her to marry a—an unmoneyed—peasant. So-she slipped Mamma's diamond brooch, worth something like a hundred-thousand dollars, American, into my overworked overnight case.

"I didn't see it," I said. "Where was it?"

"In—in the pretty little box with the tropical sunset scene, marked 'Tahiti.' "

Oh. She'd been in my bag, all right. She had certainly described the little box that had contained—

"What was in that box before, Giulia?"

"Wickedness. Three condoms, in assorted colors. I remember a blue and a sort of orangy red."

Wickedness! Yeah. Stealing her mother's brooch was OK; lying to me, presumably having my room searched and then doing it herself; screwing with her boyfriend and with me; even her parents' adulterous games—those, to Giulia Fanfani, were OK. But she was Italian, and she had almost become a nun. Thus conception preventers were-wickedness!

"Ok, what else. What if I'd found the brooch?"

She sighed, sniffling, regarding the floor, fiddling with her purse. "A-a person was to get the brooch out of your bag as soon as you were out of Italy. You—you've been watched ever since you left our villa."

"Uh-huh. Nice boyfriend you've got, Julie. I mean *had*. He must've snatched the brooch, bag and all, on the train!"

"No-no-no, he did NOT!" she whimpered, her voice rising and her shoulders shaking. "And now he has threatened ME! It was he who searched your room. And telephoned me. With a threat. I flew here immediately—I *had* to. Now I am *scared,* Lance! God, Lance—they'll KILL us!"

"They?"

"I mean he, then," she amended in a tiny voice.

"Like hell," I said, going to the telephone. "I'll call the local constabulaire, right now!" And I started to pick up the phone.

"No, Lance."

A new quality, a sort of diamond hardness in her

175

voice made me turn, slowly. Yep. It had happened, to me. For the very first time in my life. First it was a line out of a movie: "They'll KILL us!" And now it was the other thing: a gun. A pistol. Small and shiny-black and nasty looking. I could see partway into the barrel—because it was aimed at me.

Her hand quivered only a little. Even so, the pistol looked very very vicious, and I'd rather have exchanged stares with a cobra. (That stuff about their being able to *spit* venom *is* bullshit, isn't it?)

"I can't let you call the police, Lance. I'm *scared*."

"Can't—LET me! Dear God, Julie—what're you going to do, shoot me? Look, I have money—or my father does—and I don't *need* the damned brooch! But I don't need all this hassle, either."

We stared at each other for a few seconds. Then she sagged, looking very small and limp and vulnerable. I walked over and took the little pistol out of her hand. It was very cold.

We talked. At last she admitted it; she knew now that Rocco Vizzini did *not* love her, but merely wanted the brooch for himself. I had the feeling she was still lying, but I couldn't get past it.

We talked a long while. Not that we got much of anyplace, but we did play hell with that bottle of brandy. Then, forgetting all about the fact that we'd been enroute to her room, we went to bed. It was very late, and I was positively sloshing with brandy. Hell of a put-down for a naked girl in one's bed, but I think I went to sleep while using my tongue to admire her nipple. I forget which.

And when I awoke late the next morning, Giulia

Fanfani was gone. I called the desk. Giulia who?

Right. She'd never been registered.

"Jesus," I muttered, and got up to go and gulp some aspirin and B-1's. Word has it that the latter aid in the conversion of alcohol to sugar in the human system—I think that's what alcohol does. I couldn't declare under oath that they do a lot of good, but it's nice to *think* you're doing something about an alcohol-thick head, and besides they carry a built-in punishment: one's piss smells absolutely ghastly for about twenty hours!

Feeling the need of more breakfast than coffee and rolls, I went down to the dining room. There I ate well, if not heartily. I was thinking about Giulia Fanfani. And searched rooms. And stolen overnight bags. And her boyfriend. And about a missing brooch. A brooch whose disappearance coincided with my departure from the villa of Count Girolamo Fanfani!

I sincerely hoped that the thing wasn't missed for a nice long while, so that Girolamo and Elisabetta wouldn't connect me with its theft.

I decided that such things weren't worth thinking about, and furthermore that, no, I should not contact the Fanfanis and tell all. Then I returned to my room to be about the business of packing up and moving on—and broke up. I came into my room to find a different maid, and instantly on my arrival she bent over the bed in a great display of activity. Among other things.

No pants.

Chuckling, I decided against either conducting

another raid on a local store, or postponing my departure. I was soon on my way again, continuing my quest for the titivation of a tiny tingle.

CHAPTER THIRTEEN

I really hoped for better with the enormous-busted girl on the train, and I admit that balling between those juicy white watermelons of nineteen-year-old tits was something else.

So was watching her lazily, sexily grin and suck off the *eau de scrotum* I spurted over her face. Then I moved foward until I was riding those mammoth mammaries, like those plump and silky pillows old women always have in their antimacassar'd homes, and she licked and sucked until I was again imitating a flagpole, whereupon she politely asked me to dismount, after which she rolled floppily over and pushed herself up onto her hands and knees with her big Alpine ass waving in my face. Admiring her admirable attitude of healthy depravity, I plugged into the engagingly revealed slot—and I swear, she must have had a vise secreted in that damp pink sheath.

It was a jarring, straining, enervating orgasm, and I'll love her forever, whatever her name is.

But—no tingle.

My hopes were high with Lovisa, in Stockholm. She was a large and pretty young woman who wore her medium-blonde hair cut and arranged so that it showed her ears, which were tiny, eggshell pink (and just as translucent), and looked as if they wanted a healthy tonguing.

Perhaps I should mention that she was nineteen years of age, precisely six feet tall, and had three older sisters. None of them were married; each had a child. Lovisa, I swiftly learned and not unhappily, shared their propensity but didn't want the progeny. With her it was fellatio and sodomy only. For all I know, she was technically a virgin, elsewise. You don't argue with a kid that big.

Besides, the fitting of roundish peg into a round hole seems to make a great deal of sense, and it certainly is pleasant to kneel up behind a pair of big, pillowy pink, youthfully firm buttocks, and bang hell out of them with your crotch and hips, listening to the damp and pulpy sounds of her dangling tits—which were good-sized but not proportionately huge—jiggling and slapping each other beneath her. As, spurred by the heat and the tightness, and her inarticulate sounds and grunting gasps as she rocks her big form back and forth, you thrust your body's best part in and out of her body's most intimate and tight aperture. Bending forward, hunching, shoving your wincing cock through clinging layers of tight heated anal flesh, working it up and down the long tunnel to her bowels—until you inudate them with a flood of wet heat.

Marvelous!

And it sent all sorts of delightful tingles through me.

But not *the* tingle, dammit. Or maybe not dammit; it would have been worse than unfortunate to have discovered that the tingle existed only with a nineteen-year-old girl with an anti-baby hangup and a positively voracious rectum!

Besides, she spoke precisely eleven words of English, none of them well.

But this was—shaking. I had come to entertain thoughts of hatred for, and mayhem about, my father! Damn him, dear old dad had married the one woman I seemed slated for, without my even knowing it when I had her in my clutches. She was several years older than I, and now she was my stepmother.

But—dammit, with her I experienced that existential extra, that indescribable tingling sensation deep in the gut, as well as the customary one in the balls! And now, in four countries and enroute in between as well, I had found no one else who could provide that same sensational sensation!

Arrrgh!

There was a wild scene in the hotel in Oslo. Making it in the maid's closet with the best-looking maid I've ever seen. She was from *Wales,* for pete's sake, and ask me not what the hell a Welshwoman was doing maiding in a hotel in Norway. Darling, sweet little tits, and absolutely striking face, and the biggest clitoris I've ever seen, diddled, vibrated, felt explode and dive back into its sheath. As far as it could dive; she could have screwed with that thing. Maybe she did, but not me. Very enthusiastic, Very grateful. And tingle-less.

I had to assume that it was merely coincidental that someone took a cut at me with a car that same night, as I crossed the street to visit a little singles bar. No one wanted to maim or kill me, surely!

In that bar, I somehow got involved with an unmixed pair of large Norwegian sailors, and got punched up pretty well, and got dragged and or carried out by a large woman of about thirty-five. She took me home with her. Used warm compresses on my bruises, which she exposed with perfect aplomb. Then she put out the lights, undressed, and entered the bed with me. With her back turned. (It was the only bed she had.) Considerably more inebriated than titillated, and feeling an assortment of twinges and worse from some well-landed Norwegian fists, I left her back alone. And returned swiftly to sleep.

In the morning my nurse advised that I certainly radiated a lot of warmth for a slim young fellow, and that I would come in very handy on cold Norwegian nights; I advised her that she certainly was cool of skin for a er-ah big woman (the while palming her big long breasts), and in about two shakes I was being tugged onto and into her. We were both appreciative, I am sure, although I discovered a couple of painful bruises and stiff muscles I'd forgotten about. More twinge than tingle. No tingle at all. Just extraordinary vigor and enthusiasm, a lot of flesh, a lot of flesh-splatting, sweaty screwing and hard breathing, and a superb come. Excellent woman, Gertrud.

Some guy trailed me out of her apartment building and all the way to the hotel. I didn't know if it was a husband, a lover, or worse still, one of those scabrous sailors, who were sickeningly *strong* dudes. Or maybe Giulia's boyfriend? Or Giulia in reverse drag?

I got on a plane as fast as possible and got the hell out of Norway, but the flamenco dancer in the night-club-tourist-trap in Lisbon, while a fiery and excellent companion in bed, slapped me silly with her wild successive movements and gave me no tingles—except from the scratches she clawed into my back.

And the American girl I tried to pick up slugged me with her purse. I should have known better! Americans, after all!

After that brief episode I sat very chastened at my little table, suffering the stinging stares of outraged patrons, trying to pretend interest in my drink and in the music while wishing I could somehow absent myself from the scene of my downfall and humiliation, without slinking. Then this unmadeup, longhaired, bespectacled chick came over.

She was wearing a loosely hanging satin dress over loosely swinging breasts and very American pantyhose. She came on with a bit of pidgin Portuguese, which I started to answer back in my half-ass Spanish, then changed my mind. I responded in Amerenglish.

She laugehd. "You're American!"

I nodded. "An ugly one, doubtless. You, too? American I mean, not ugly."

"Um, yeah. I'm here on a grant-thing. You know. Supposed to be studying art. Gotten into sociology, though. I was trying to apologize for that bitch—that ugly American who slugged you. Poor man. What'd you do, pinch her?"

"Tried to pick her up. That's absolutely all. I do not pinch."

"Hm. How are you on spanking?"

"Beg pardon?"

She sighed and gave her long loose hair a toss; it was dark yellowish blonde, hadn't been shampooed too recently, and clung slickly together. "I asked how, if you don't pinch, you are on spanking?"

"Never thought much about it," I admitted. "I wouldn't care to have the experience, thanks. My father used to wallop me, but not much, and that was a long time . . ."

She giggled; pretty face, very pretty when she smiled. Nice teeth. Her eyes were extra-large behind her glasses, gray-blue. "I didn't mean getting spanked, man! I mean I feel, like, into helping out a fellow American in distress. You know. Like a horny and good-looking male, and I just wondered if we got off on the same things. I like being spanked."

"On the bottom?"

"Where else do you get spanked?"

"I don't get spanked anywhere," I assured her. "And—gee, I'm not too sure about doing it, either. I mean—I never have."

She looked incredulous. "You a virgin, man?"

"Uh-uh," I said, shaking my head. That was enough.

Her clinging hair brushed her shoulders as she shook her head. "Wow. And you've never met someone who's into being, like, spanked, huh?" She favored me with an almost pitying smile. "You probably have, but just didn't know it, I'll bet. Lots of people are. Do, I mean. In England it's mostly the men who want to be spanked. But I guess a lot of people are too uptight to admit it, that's why I say you must have known some without knowing it."

"Uh, yeah."

"I just thought I'd, you know, ask."

"Well, sit down, fella'merrican, lay your name on me, and let's talk about it."

She didn't drink, she assured me, but she did sit down and lay her name on me: Estelle Wcejak, and I was never able to duplicate her pronunciation.

She had a fine tight ass with large roundish cheeks that jiggled when she walked, and she was fine ass. With her sort of—directing, I spanked her quite a bit. And with me sort of directing, we sucked and sexed and sodomized and whatever else we thought of, during the three days I stayed with her, totally fascinated with her. My hand always got sore before her needy tail did, though. I even took her to a hotel and checked us in and we bathed together—her dumpy apartment didn't have a bath, and the damned "convenience" down the hall was *always* in use—and we washed her hair. And then I spanked her, with her across my knees while I sat on the toilet. (With the seat down; let us not indicate too much, ah, perversity.) She came before I quit, that time, because I started using the sole of one of her sandals and didn't have to worry about my hand starting to sting. Then she slid off my lap, all damp and sighing with her climax, and knelt there and sucked me off.

Spanking is sort of fun, although it does make the hand sore, and I guess I recommend that everyone *try* it, else how do you know whether you're missing out on the big thrill Estelle got from it?

Her hair dried during the night and coiled up into a lovely aggregation of waves and curls. When I awoke, she was still fast asleep, and I stared at her. I was shaken. She was beautiful. Just lovely. And I was really getting high on her. Our sex was good; our talking was good. A nutty girl, very young but thinking with the arrogance of the very young that she had the answers, all of them, and into doing nutty things because she thought you should always do or say just what you felt like, from one instant to the next.

She's probably right, too.

It palls on you after awhile, somebody like that. Yet Estelle was beautiful, and we made it beautifully together; she had no sexual hangups that showed, unless you count the desire—the need—to be spanked. A fine sexual appetite. And I was fascinated with her. Which was bad. I was in danger of falling in love with Estelle—despite the lack of tingle—and I knew it. I also knew that we would be miserable. She was what Jung called a sensation type, a *pure* sensation type, overlaid or diluted with nothing. I'm probably wrong, but to me that's like being twelve years old, *all* the time.

So I got up, dressed, packed, and went AWOL. Estelle was still decoratively asleep in my hotel room bed, looking too beautiful and scarily desirable and—fascinating.

I paid the room ahead two days and got the hell out of Portugal.

Back to France, from whence I was due to sail in three days. I spent that time, believe it or not, playing tourist. Hell, I'd never *seen* Montmartre, or Mouline Rouge, or the little dump where Mau-Mau Utrillo was supposed to have lived, painting the pictures he traded for brandies at the nearest watering spot, poor super-talented bastard (He was, you know. Both—).

Then I was going up the gangplank, heading home and thinking sadly that it was all over. But it wasn't.

CHAPTER FOURTEEN

Getting on a ship is and always has been a fun-thing, and it is a shame that airplanes are pretty much wiping out sea travel.

Going by boat is not just a means of transporta-tion; it is a social phenomenon, a social thing, and a status thing as well. There is time to get to *know* your fellow travelers—I think it's OK to start using that phrase again, with Senator McCarthy long since discredited and dead—because you all pretty much live together for whatever time it is; a week, a couple of weeks (traveling on a ship makes one feel like calling it a fortnight, and pronouncing it Britishly: fortn't), or longer.

Usually when you get on a plane you wonder about some of the other passengers. Some of them look interesting, or you overhear bits and pieces of interesting coversations. But air travel is a structured thing; it *is* travel, and that's all, no matter how hard the airlines try to make it seem social by training their flight attendants and serving you this and that. And the only way you get to "know" anyone else on an airplane is if you are alone and sit next to someone else who is, or someone sits next to you. But that is what you do on a plane; you *sit*. Anything you want is brought to you, unless you have to go; that's about the extent of your getting up. And if you're in choppy skies and the FASTEN SEAT BELTS sign is lighted, and your body manifests a desire to avail itself to the airborne bathroom facilities—tough! Sure, maybe it's urgent, a clamorous cry from the bladder, and you can unstrap and even make your lurching way to the little room. But you're going to be challenged by a flight attendant, who has suddenly become not your friendly neighborhood overdressed bunny, but the Warder of the Gates of Establishment.

Sure she has a job to do; sure you might fall and bash your 'ead in. But such chances become worth taking when your eyeballs begin to turn yellow and you feel the pressure way up in your chest!

But the subject at hand is ocean travel, and more *specifically,* my trip back to the U.S. of A. on board the *Carcosa*. And the fact that entirely sufficient opportunities exist for one to meet the other passengers, unless one is really an indrawn sort—or too far in the opposite direction, for we all tend to look down up and shun the hyper-gregarious types.

Some interesting people sailed with me. There was the Texican oil millionaire, Loren Buford Jenkins; LBJ to his friends, he announced, and he wanted everyone to be his friend. Sorry, no cliché; his part would *not* be played by Phil Harris. The guy was big, sure, but plain as a stick. Wore things like whipcords and just plain old shirts. Normal belts and boots, not those execrable blond-leather waist-straps with the enormous buckles and high heeled boots we associate with denizens of the Lone Star State. A nice quiet guy, who played one hell of a lot of cards all the way home. I thought it was probably poker. Turned out to be a game called Spades, a sort of cross between Hearts and Bridge without the stupidity of the former's having one 13-point card, and without the necessity of concentration of the latter, that aspect of bridge that makes it a bloody predator's game, to my thinking. I heard he and his fellow card-freaks played for a penny a point.

Then there was his daughter. Mousy little thing, very slender, with a fall of the most beautiful jet-black hair I've ever seen. And dark eyes to match, eyes made strange by her slight squint. Her cheeks were beautified by the deepest dimples I've ever seen. It was a great experience, to see her smile. Her name was Lola Belle Jenkins. Uh-huh. LBJ, junior. She wore her raven hair loose, and wrapped her body in things like gingham shirts and jeans, probably bought at Nieman-Marcus at the cost of a tailor-made suit.

There were the Duke and Duchess of Offa.

Britishers, both tall, he very slim and she absolutely voluptuously constructed. Wore her red hair bunned, and the bun was big, indicating she had quite a lot of hair. It made you wonder—that and her luxurious figure—what it might look like down, loose, caressing her shoulders in a mane of flame. They looked to be about forty, and each of them was a young forty. Both dressed like what they were, too, British nobility. I had the feeling that Alfred, Duke of Offa most probably wore a necktie with his pajamas. They dressed for dinner each evening, members of the old school, people who *belonged* on that liner. And I mean *dressed;* dinner clothes for 'is lordship, perfectly-tied bow tie and black studs and so on, and floor-length gowns for 'is lady. (Leddy, that's the proper spelling to show the pronunciation.) They did have magnificent accents, the upper-teeth-forward type. Come to think, both were equipped with large teeth. Of more interest, admittedly, were the large jugs her leddyship was equipped with. Tossing great footballs that appeared to be mounted on springs.

They were traveling with a black maid, a girl from Martinique. Very decorative, and not, of course, black at all *Cafe-au-lait,* is the phrase, nicely creamed coffee.

In addition to these there was a French marquis with a broke look about him. Interesting man. Had a pair of canines that made you wonder if his ancestors mightn't have come from Transylvania. He, too, was traveling with a daughter, a young-looking one (by that I mean twenty or less). Her blouse always appeared to be buttoned precariously over the convallariaceous curvature of her nicely pointed breasts. They were decidedly delectable, those wideset pointy breasts, and so were the nicely divided halves of her backside, fleshy globes that thrust audaciously out to follow her everywhere, working beautifully in their efforts to keep up.

And then there was the veiled woman. I mean a *heavily* veiled woman. The veil was black; so were her clothes. I saw her when I was boarding, and was instantly fascinated; she had a young look about her, and her legs were very nice indeed. Unfortunately she kept totally to herself. I did learn, with the exercise of a little craft, that she was signed on as Signora la Contessa di Pina. Obviously a widow in deep mourning for poor departed Signore il Conti di Pina.

We met at dinner the third night out, the Duke and Duchess and I. The previous night they had supped at the captain's table. Now a bit of democracy had set in, and here we were, me beside the Duchess, he on her other side, a young French couple on his right—very taken with each other; probably honeymooning, I decided—and then a young ship's officer named Dumas. No, he advised, no kin.

The dinner was good and the conversation fair; it was the Duke, the officer, and yours truly, the only American at the table, who did most of it. I thought that the Duke was making eyes at Lola Belle Jenkins, who was at the next table wearing some sort of flowered tent who's only redeeming quality was that it was clingy. But I couldn't be sure, and besides I was preoccupied. Within a few minutes after we'd all seated and introduced ourselves. I felt the pressure of a large and notably warm leg against my right leg. I considered moving it, but decided to let it stay where it was. The Duchess had encountered me, doubtless by accident; why should I apologize and jerk away.

But either it was not by accident or she had no feeling in that gloriously warm thigh. The pressure increased. The Duke was addressing himself to me, talking about the recent strengthening of the Amedican dollah and what it meant to the United Kingdom. Leaning forward just a bit, in order to talk across his wife, who seemed a most silent and withdrawn woman indeed. But now her improprietous thigh was moving. Just a bit. Caressing my leg. I glanced at her. And missed his next several sentences; she winked! I blinked. And moved my own thigh a bit, her way. It was soon being fondled, dangerously close to the crucual area, and my mind labored under the ambivalent feelings; I was unsure whether to be glad or sad she wasn't left-handed. Had she been, she'd not have had it available to muck about with my leg in manner distinctly naughty, whilst she sat calmly and rather affectedly eating in manner distinctly haughty.

With my ambivalent reaction? Because she was affecting not only my mental equilibrium but the state of relaxation of my best parts. It was, in fact, becoming unmistakably unrelaxed. Turning into a veritable horn that entertained thoughts of its own about placing a set of horns on her husband's lordly head. But how could I possibly assume that the indelicate pursuits of this noblewoman's flagrant fingers amounted to anything else than a dinner-table amusement that would swiftly end with the destruction of the dessert? After all, she was coming on for being forty or more, and there sat her husband beside her, talking away, a peer of the realm who looked as if he wouldn't be caught dead possessing anything so gross as desire, much less the erection she was forcing upon me.

Maybe that's it, I mused, trying hard to listen to what the French officer was saying to the duke. Maybe Alfie isn't giving Maudie enough—that's what they called each other, Alfie and Maudie— and she was exploring the possibility of improving both the sorry state of her libido and Anglo-American relations.

Lifting my wine glass with my left hand, I slipped my right down to touch hers. Instantly her fingers coiled over and around like half and octopus, gripping my fingers, and tickling my palm.

"Oh, they do that in England, too, eh?" I asked, nonplussed but trying to cover.

"Whot?" her husband asked, bending a bit forward.

"Yes," she drawled quietly, without looking up from her plate. Hers was an excellent appetite. Obviously a goodly amount of food would be required, to keep the fires burning in her amplitudinous anatomy. And the fires were certainly burning!

"Oh," the Duke said, "pardon me—the gentleman was addressing you?"

She nodded, favoring my tremulous hand with a last squeeze and then allowing it to go on about its business. Which was getting hurriedly back onto the table.

"Soddy," Alfred of Offa said, "I hadn't heahd you say anything, my deah."

"I didn't, Alfred," his wife advised him equably. "His query was elicited by my tickling his palm."

I began to wonder about the availability of Alka-Seltzer on the *Carcosa*. My stomach did a half-gainer at her words, then came down hard. *Good,* I thought distressedly, *Gawd!*

"Oh yes," he said, just as blandly as she, "of course. Oh, by the way, the gentleman from, ahh, Texas has ahsked me to his stateroom latah, foah a bit of cahds. I do hope you won't mind being left alone this evening Maudie deah."

"No," she said evenly, "nawt a tawl, deah. I shall ahsk Mistah Holliman to escawt me to ouah stateroom, and since I feel a bit moah in need of bed than cahds, I am suah I shall soon be curled up with something—interesting."

Although presumably, or at least hopefully, the other three persons at our table thought she was referring to a book, the words brought the heads of the young French couple together. Both their hands then disappeared beneath the table; they became a bit agitated, and shortly they were excusing themselves. The Duchess smiled. We, however, tarried long enough to have dessert and a smoke. Then, brandy in hand, the duke took his leave of us and meandered off in the direction of Texas. Lady Maude and I bade our final dinner companion a good night and we wended our way off in the direction of England. We did not, however, meander; she set a brisk pace and I hung right in there.

"Would you like a drink, Mistah Holliman?" she asked, once we were in their cabin. "A brandy, perhaps, a sherry?"

"A brandy sounds lovely," I told her, "but I do think your calling me 'Mister Holliman' is ridiculous, milady."

She chuckled. "How quaint 'milady' sounds!" She went over to where several bottles reposed. "But you force an admission from me, then—I don't recall your first name."

"Lance," I said. "I hope you feel we know each other well enough for you to use it." I noted that my enunciation and choice of words were taking on a decidedly British bent.

"Well," she said, bending over slightly as she poured brandy into a handsome pair of snifters, each bearing gold rim and a coat of arms, "if we don't know each other well enough, we soon will, now won't we?"

My reply was physical, not vocal; I went over to stand behind her with my snug-flied trousers pressed against the broad, twinned swell of her estimable arse. My hande wandered over her ribcage and hips, and she bumped backward in a way that made me gasp.

She turned grinning, making sure she stayed within the half-circle of my hands. Her large bust dented my jacket. She smiled, a large handsome woman with a brandy snifter in each hand.

"Well, you impetuous young American! How you take advantage—and just when I find myself with both hands full, so that I am utterly helpless to prevent your sliding my gown even farther off my shoulders!"

I did that.

They were large, well-rounded shoulders, and the tops of the breasts I revealed were similarly rounded and large. They rose higher, forced upward by the pressure of their extremities against me as she leaned forward and raised her lips to mine. I met it halfway, striving to keep from swallowing the tongue she sent almost violently into my mouth. We and the brandy warmed up considerably, my hands rising and rising until I was pushing even more of her towering tits up out of her lowered dress. Then I ducked my head to implant a kiss in their cleavage, a great dark crevasse that tried to steam my eyeballs with their radiant warmth. Her sigh was throaty, almost a growl.

Eventually we got ourselves over to the bed, where we sat side by side and let our hands engage in unabashed sexuality while we sniffed and sipped our (excellent) cognac. I had soon discovered a tractable zipper, whose owner tractably arched her back to facilitate its downward flight. Then I was gazing at a brazen black bra with cups of a size sufficient to accommodate bowling balls. Perhaps that's an unfortunate comparison, bowling balls being both hard and black, while the swollen-looking breasts spilling out of her bra like melting ice cream were definitely both soft and vanilla in appearance.

Watching me with semi-veiled eyes, vouchsafing me a closed-mouth smile, she lifted her snifter slowly to her lips—and squeezed the evergrowing bulge of my pants.

"Milady," I said, "you have quite the biggest breasts I have ever seen."

She laughed, squeezing harder. "What a wonderful thing to say! What mahvelous, uttahly *naughty* language! Tell me moah!"

Thus encouraged, I said, "I should like nothing more than to bring forth those vast British beachballs and suckle at their doubtless swollen tips like a child!"

She laughed again, genuinely, and tossed off the rest of her brandy. Since she looked as if she were about to toss off the snifter, too, and since it was so handsome, I took it from her and set it on the bedside table beside the phone and the paperback book there. The book, by the way, was *Frannie's Fanny,* which is more meaningful when you consider that "fanny" is the English word for "cunt"

By the time I had turned back to her, she had the several catches at the back of her bra open. The black holster slipped off the bulging upper slopes of her heroic jugs and fell down until her broad, flaring hips slowed its progress. Her suddenly-exposed breasts flopped and bounced. Melting ice cream? More like bowls of white Jell-o. I had to stare, in some awe, at the sheer beauty of those boobs. They were astonishingly smooth, symmetrical, elongated half-globes studded low down with enticing roseate nipples.

"And does one still admire my—my vast British beachballs, Lance? Hardly a *girl's* bosom, you know, not so firm, as they were in my salad days."

"Your salad days," I told her gallantly and dry-throatedly, "are still with you, milady." I strained my back in bending forward to press a kiss onto first one, then the other large nipple.

"How nice," she purred. "But you'd bettah stop calling me 'milady,' Sir Lancelot. Shall I be Guinevere?"

"You shall be balled!"

"Does that mean tupped?"

"Screwed!"

"That's the same as fucked, isn't it?"

"Quite!"

"Quite," she agreed, and got up to get rid of the rest of her clothes.

She handled that very swiftly, baring a good broad and convex belly that sent a line of red hair downward like a creeper that erupted into a glossy jungle between the tops of her full thighs. Then we attacked my clothing, the two of us, and I was soon just as naked, rudely pointing at her with a precociously swollen phallus that hadn't let off its steam in nearly a week. She seized upon it. I seized upon her titanic tits. We collapsed onto the bed. We mauled each other, and when I began sucking, she twisted herself about and began treating my cockhead like an outsized nipple. I was striving to stuff my mouth with the great dangling fruits of her knockers, and she was meanwhile striving just as assiduously to stuff her face with my rampant masculinity. She sighed, reveling in all of it, and her nipples stiffened and swelled still more, seemingly imitating my cock, and ran out into long projections that I pulled deep into my mouth.

Most unusual, to put it Britishly: her nipples were obviously as sensitive as my penis. We came together!

But Maude kept my ignoble dork in her noble mouth, and kept right on sucking and running her mouth up and down the soft flesh, and so I returned my attentions to her big pillowy breasts, and then to her fur, which was soft and hot and moist, and she twitched and groaned and kept on working away at me. And gradually throbbing, my penis became a cock again, rigid and thick under her action and the caressing, tantalizing pressures and glide of her persistent mouth and wriggly tongue. I felt my scrotum tightening, felt not spurts of renewed vigor and desire, knew that it was a larger and larger morsel of my flesh that was snugly clamped in the luscious, clinging, wet warmth of her face.

They don't tell . . . they don't swell . . . and they're grateful as hell. . . . Who said that about making it with older women; was it Franklin? I didn't know, and I didn't care. The words had run across my mind in Italy, and now there they were again. Snotty damned words! I was already changing my mind about what is "old" and what is "desirable." So we all go out in search of shapely young chicks, hmmm? Wow, I now think, the *smart* cocksman could get in twice as much of his favorite activity, and probably enjoy it a lot more and get his male ego hoisted withal, by *ignoring* those shapely young chickybabies and going after the world's large supply of available women over forty!

Suddenly Maude relinquished her oral hold on my new-grown erection. She practically flung herself backward, on her back, and those big meaty, white thighs splayed wide. Her big cushiony bosom jumped and rippled as she thrust out her arms to me.

"Now, now Sir Lancelot, my knight—*now screw me properly!*"

"Let's do it—*im*properly," I grunted, getting swiftly into the big V of her legs and, with the aid of one of her hot hands, driving my spike home and instantly beginning the attempt to nail her to her stateroom bed.

And yes, absolutely yes, make no mistake: that was a good, a truly superb and memorable *fuck!* Her body was a marvelous cushion under mine, all soft and increasingly damp, just as her interior was. That up-rounded, heaving belly and fantastic bosom were shaken with violent shudders of passion—and with her own wild attempts to move like an eighteen-year-old sylph rather than a forty-year-old nymph. I drove in hard and deep, and she squirmed to facilitate her own imparadising impalement. She groaned and her body trembled when my hands slithered in beneath her, grasping at the big voluptuous curves of her buttocks. Up came her legs; apart came those great cheeks; down came her calves to catch me in a squeeze play. I responded by skewering her with a stiffened finger in her noble arse.

"Ah," she gasped out, her eyes bulging, "ah! I haven't—felt that thrill for—ah—twenty years. . . . Push, push, *push,* my marvelous lover!"

So I pushed, impaling her fore and aft simultaneously, screwing her from both directions at once, both warm sheaths filled and sliding on hard shafts.

We both made it again, and she and I had a very fine time (while, as I later discovered, her lordly husband was balling also, with Lola Belle Jenkins of Arlington, Texas), but—I won't say it. Thank God, though! If I *had* tingled with Maude, Duchess of Offa, I *would* have been in trouble!

The following afternoon it seemed to be my turn, or something, with LBJ junior, and it was in my cabin that Lola Belle and I got together.

We played around a lot, messing, kissing, stroking, just playing and then, lying on the bed, grinning. I told her I wanted her naked, which state she achieved while I watched. Next I told her I wanted me naked, too, and she took care of that also, dragging off my clothing with more uninhibited enthusiasm than expertise.

A distraction arose at that time; I seemed to have lost one of my fingers, and she hunched there in a position somewhere between a sit and a squat, moaning and rolling her head and riding that vanished finger. Meanwhile my equipment saluted her from between my thighs, rearing beneath her with its eyelike opening seeming to study her interestedly in a lecherous gaze. The exodus of my finger from her drooling genital orifice was followed by a low cry, after which she practically bounded astride me.

I lay there like a lazy sultan and grinned up at her as, with her feet planted wide astride me, she lowered herself.

In moments she was riding me unmercifully, writhing with sensuous sexuality. Her wild movements bounced her pretty breasts and made her hair fly and swirl about her shoulders, a dense cloud of pure black. But I watched her breasts, mostly, heaving in tumultuous excitement, bouncing wildly, their aroused peaks jutting and seeming to draw invisible pictures in the air as they danced furiously before her. And she seemed such a quiet, mousey girl! Not bloody likely; her body was obviously afire with an intensity of passion and pure enjoyment that had her moving faster, ever faster. Riding like she was a cowgirl aboard the mechanical bull at Gilley's. . . .

"YAAA-HOOOOOOOO!" she cried, just as I had that cowgirl thought, and scared me out of a future day or two of my life. "HOOOO—PEEEEE!" she cried out again, swinging her right arm like a pump-handle.

But it wasn't a horse she flailed with her imaginary crop, and fortunately it wasn't her human mount, either: me. She was slapping her own right hip and nicely rounded flank!

All she needed was a ten-gallon hat, the idiot. Instead, she got something like ten gallons of my juices, and after that she settled down and became quiet again. She didn't have anything to say, that Texican temptress. She just liked to fornicate, which is saying a lot, I reckon.

Fortunately the tingle hadn't been there, nor was it present when the black maid from Martinique and I made it on the floor of her employers' stateroom. While, unbeknownst to me, her employers were napping in the next room. Nice. Also unequivocally shaking, when you learn that you could have been interrupted at any second. There's definitely a lot to be said for making it *quietly!*—also with someone of much darker skin. The contrast is beautiful. It's a bit of too bad, this racial thing. You see quite a few black guys with white girlfriends in cities and on campuses. The girls are usually blonde. They're sort of into the current American game, liberal chic: See? See? *I'm* not a bigot, I'm not prejudiced, ain't that marvy and ain't I *something,* though! And in his case I more than suspect it's a sort of HA-gotcha-whitey! sort of thing? You shades've been dumping on me and mine for years and years, whitey—now I've got me this honky chick,and it's *her* idea, baby, and how's *that* grab you? But—you just don't see the other side of the coin very often. White male, black female. Because the psychological reasons just aren't there? Because the white males might be a little scared? Because the black females have more pride and less to prove?

I can't be sure. Maybe Carl Jung or Fritz Perls or Eric Berne could have helped—but they are all three dead, dammit. Meanwhile, though, it's sort of a shame. Because once again: the contrast, the constant awareness and noticing and getting off on differences between our skins was an artistic addition to my balling with Marjorie, which was the unfortunately un-exotic name of the young woman from Martinique. I think we both enjoyed it. Aesthetic appreciation, an extra added attraction for what was, for both of us, a lovely interlude.

Without a tingle, of course.

I say *of course* because by this time I was used to it. Maybe not quite resigned, but getting close. At least I didn't have the feeling of exasperation anymore; desolation was more like it. Then I'd kick myself around, mentally, for being such a picky demanding bastard, all this balling and I wasn't satisfied. Like a kid raised on candy who doesn't get the specific *kind* he wants. But—once you've tasted the kind of candy mommy and daddy eat, out of a box with those pretty little black crenelated cups— you can *eat* mallo-cups, but they're never quite the same. Not quite as good. Nice, but—a little something missing. Like a damned tingle in the guts.

At least no one searched my cabin.

I had this strange feeling, and I kept asking around about the veiled woman . . . Contessa di Pina. No one could help, and those who perhaps could, would not. I even tried bribery, but the steward wasn't susceptible either to money or to my little suggestions concerning Lola Bell Jenkins. I think he was already making it with her, dammit.

So one day I was ambling along past the shuffleboard deck-place, and I was hailed:

"M'sieu! Would it be that you would care to make the shuffleboard with me?"

It was the French marquis with the bored look about him, except that just then he wasn't looking bored at all, but old-world sharp in white sweater

205

and (full-cut) white trousers and a beat-up pair of sneakers. And he was smiling, flashing those Draculesque canines at me. (I glanced up. Plenty of sun, and there he was. No, he was OK, not a member of the Undead, unless Stoker had screwed up his researches and vampires *could* stand the sunlight.)

I thought what the hell, and we played shuffleboard. In most friendly fashion. And he beat the tar out of me. Twice.

"I think we've proven that shuffleboard isn't my game, M'sieu le Marquis," I chuckled, after the second disaster. "Drinking's not exactly my game either, but I could use one. May the vanquished buy the victor a drink in a nice dark cool bar?"

His smile flashed—he wasn't a bad-looking man at all, and had certainly retained his figure; too bad he hadn't thought about having those teeth filed off a bit—but then he pushed up his sweater sleeve to reveal a sweat-glistening wrist and a watch with an impressively handsome band. He made a little moue and gave his head a single swift shake.

"It lacks ten minutes of being five," he said, "and at five I am to meet my daughter in the bar. I regret that—unless you would care to join us, M'sieu Holliman?"

"I'd be delighted," I said truthfully. "I think any male on board would be happy to join your daughter, anywhere."

"Most kind," he said in an old-world fashion, and we set aside our sticks and moved barward. There were two on the *Carcosa*, The Carcose Lounge and The Taproom, which makes one wonder about the imagination of the mental giant who came up with the names. We wended our way Taproomward.

"You have been in my country on business, M'sieu?" the marquis asked, once we were in that nice cool, dimly-lit bar and had ordered; he had decided to join me in a gin and tonic, which is the most cooling drink I know of.

"No, my lord, I . . ."

"Please call me Baudel, won't you—the family name."

"Thank you," I said, thinking how nice it was that I had met so many nobles of assorted countries who had such definite tendencies toward democracy. "At any rate, I have been merely wandering. In truth, my father was recently married for the second time, and I felt that all three of us were better off with me elsewhere for a time." I smiled. "Too, he gave me a handsome check, sort of as a reverse-wedding gift. I'm afraid I haven't done anything important or seen much to brag about. Nor, come to think, have I taken any pictures. I am more interested in people, and have been spending most of my time, observing and talking." *And balling,* I thought, but I certainly didn't see how I could drop that on him! "Now that it's brought up, I feel almost embarrassed, like a tourist on one of those 'if this is Thursday, this must be Paris' package deals. I've been to Rome, Florence and a villa outside, Stockholm, Oslo, Nice, Lisbon . . . and finally in Paris. There I admit I did succumb to tourister tendencies, and spent a good deal of time wandering around the Montmartre area."

207

He was smiling, nodding. Long thin face with sensuous lips and a very slender nose. Dark eyes, black hair, worn combed back and a bit too heavily pomaded. Handsome hands, slim and long-fingered; the kind of hands that make some people approach a total stranger and ask if he is an artist (and he turns out to be a garage mechanic, because what the hell do hands have to do with anything)?

"Yes, yes, I see. You are single, then?"

I nodded, then sat back while our drinks were set before us. We both said thank you to the steward, and then each of us exchanged a look of respect and camaraderie. He lifted his drink.

"To politeness to the help," he suggested.

I nodded and we drank. "And—to the victor go the spoils," I added, and the marquis—that is, Baudel—laughed, making a little deprecatory gesture that relegated shuffleboard into the realm of the absolutely unimportant.

"Your pardon, M'sieu Holliman, but—you are accustomed to money, then."

I blinked. Put my head on one side, thought about it, and at last gave him a nod. He was making an apologetic face and gesture.

"An unfortunate question," he said, rather hastily. "I do apologize. It was just your manner with the servant. People who are not accustomed to having them around are inevitably either rude or too ingratiating, as though they are afraid the experience will suddenly blow away."

"Good," I said, leaning forward, "that's good, and excellent observation, Baudel! And it's just as obvious you are accustomed to your role, too . . .

you have used the word 'help' and the word 'servant,' but not 'steward' or 'waiter.'"

He studied me, looking slightly distressed. "Is that not good? One should call them steward and waiter?"

"No, one should call them whatever one thinks. But in my country so few people have servants, and there is no tradition of nobility, that we use the specific words rather than the general."

He considered that, as if rolling it around over his tongue like a wine-taster. "Hm. One learns. And what does M'sieu call his help?"

"Martha," I said, and he blinked, staring for a moment, and then we both laughed. Which was when his daughter joined us. We rose for her and the introductions, a couple of father-daughter things were said, and the waiter-I-mean-servant was there before I could summon him. The young Frenchwoman looked at her father.

"Do you think I dare have one of the American martinis, father?"

He shrugged, smiling indulgently. "One *can* be too careful, Suzanne. And Mister Holliman is, I assure you, a gentleman."

I wondered what that had to do with it, but not for long.

"Martini, *s'il vous plait,*" the pretty brunette told the waiter, who made a brief bow that involved his head and body simultaneously. As he departed she turned to me, dark eyes dancing: "Martinis make me sexy," she confided.

That was a bit sticky, and I probably didn't handle it very well, what with her dad right there. And her stuffed blouse pointing my way, as usual seeming to strain at its buttons. She also had a perfectly lovely mouth, much like her father's but pleasantly and very definitely feminine.

"I know exactly what you mean," I said. "That's why I never drink them at parties. Besides, the third one makes me sleepy."

She laughed, and we had our drink and chatted. I learned that Suzanne Baudel was en route to the States to meet and marry a new-wealthy Wall Streeter. The reason, I decided, was money, and I was reminded of the money-hunting Constanza di Stresa, back in Rome.

What a shame, I mused; Suzanne seemed so nice and unspoiled. I suppose millions of others before her had been. Look up Isabella of Jerusalem sometime, there was a sad mess of a life—or for the matter of that, Lucrezia, the pawn of her Borgia brother and the Borgia Pope Alexander. Women as chattel. Marriage as a means of uniting houses—or of uniting a House with a fortune.

We got along well, all three of us. Eventually we had to toddle along to get dressed for dinner. When I arrived at the dining salon I was swiftly approached by a radiant Suzanne, and advised that the three of us were at a table together. Presumably the Marquis had fixed that. I'm afraid the three of us pretty much ignored the other trio at our table, although the two teachers certainly were thrilled about meeting a genuine French Marquis. One of them was very attractive, too.

Oddly, Suzanne and I spent a lot of time talking about the Crusades. This stemmed naturally from my apologetically asking about the source of the Baudel title, which the marquis then explained; it had been conferred after the Second Crusade, the so-called King's Crusade during which Richard *coeur-de-lion* made such a name for himself. I swiftly learned that Richard had rather a different sort of reputation in France than we've got from Sir Walter Scott. It was interesting to hear them talk about him; a big burly domineering turd of a fellow who was, unfortunately or fortunately as the case may be, absolutely superb at both tactics and combat. But it was Philip Augustus of *France* he had insulted, and obviously the Baudels felt that Guy de Lusignan was the less worthy choice for King of Jerusalem than Philip's choice, Conrad. They didn't think Richard's conduct, once he was back in England after his Austrian captivity and had got John off the throne, was too cool, either (he immediately sailed back to his French provinces, where he remained, warring, and where he died with a crossbow quarrel through him—blood poisoning, probably).

It was a fascinating conversation, and I wished I had met Suzanne earlier and elsewhere, and that she wasn't sailing to marry a man she'd met once. A contractual arrangement, for Crissakes.

Eventually the marquis allowed the two teachers to have their innings with him, and allowed them to inveigle him into a few hands of bridge, too. Suzanne and I betook ourselves right back to The Taproom, where I asked her what she'd like.

"A martini," she said, almost desultorily.

"But they make you sexy," I reminded her, smiling, wondering why she seemed saddened but working on it.

"I know," she said meeting my eyes with her rather desolate dark ones, and I gazed at her awhile, then told the waiter we'd like two brandy-sodas.

"A martini," Suzanne said firmly.

"Two brandies-and-soda for Monsieur and one martini for Mademoiselle?"

"Suzanne . . ." I began.

"I won't rape you, Lance," she said quietly. And sadly.

"One of each," I told the waiter, and then had to explain that.

I got my brandy-soda. She got her martini. We talked. And talked. More about the Crusades. I brought up Isabella. Yes, Suzanne knew about her. A terribly sad thing; someone should write about her. A tragedy. Obviously the poor girl *liked* the rather effeminate boy she'd been betrothed to at eight and had then married, but what the hell did she have to say about it when politics came along? So first she was married off to Conrad, once her husband was gotten rid of on a ridiculous excuse, in order to give Conrad a claim on the title. Then someone had eliminated Conrad—at Saladin's or Richard's orders, who knows; Suzanne thought Richard, and I still believe it must have been Saladin, although Richard was certainly delighted—and so poor Isabella was married off again. She was pregnant by Conrad at the time of the wedding, which took place one week after Conrad's death! She was about twenty at the time. Married three times and widowed once. Just a crown with a body attached, and a conveniently placed hole in it.

Suzanne leaked a few tears over poor Isabella . . . or perhaps over poor Suzanne. She also became mildly sexy, but then as we sat there and talked and continued drinking, she also became first high and then low and then asleep.

I returned her to her cabin, had a steward let us in and then stand there while I arranged her, still clothed but shoeless, in her bed. Then he and I left together, with him doubtless wondering what sort of damned fool I was.

If ever there was a woman ready to be taken advantage of, it was the strikingly pretty and shapely one we had just left!

I considered going back for another drink but decided I didn't need it; I was tired and a bit sad, myself. I went to bed, and shortly after that, to sleep. I dreamed in full color. Of the Second Crusade: Acre. I know it would put off Sir Walter Scott something awful, but I am very much afraid that I slew Richard the Lion-Hearted.

CHAPTER FIFTEEN

I was pretty damned miserable when I got off that ship. I don't want to talk much about the why of it, either. But I'll put down a little, briefly.

The day after I put, rather than took, Suzanne Baudel to bed, her father came upon me while I was not-enjoying a flagrantly late breakfast. With his beautiful super-politeness, he apologized for interrupting me; asked diffidently if he might talk a moment, and thanked me for my kindness in allowing it. Then he thanked me for having taken such good care of his daughter, and for being such a gentleman.

I gave him a straightforward look and a statement to match: "I admit it wasn't easy, Baudel."

He nodded. "I know. Nor is *she* very happy

about it," he said quietly, letting me know he knew that I wasn't. "But if you are so inclined, Lancelot my friend, she is of course ill today and would love to have your company in her cabin, whenever you can."

After thinking about that for a few moments, I said, "Dangerous."

"You are an extraordinarily honest man, Lacelot Holliman."

"Sometimes," I told him. "When I am aware that I am not nearly the gentleman you think I am."

"Well," Paul Baudel, Marquis de Verchamp said, rising, "perhaps gentlemen are vastly over-rated in this modern world." And he went on his way.

Thirty minutes later I was knocking on Suzanne's door; she was in bed and fifteen minutes later I was sitting on it with her, and we were not talking; some few minutes after that I was in bed with her.

We left that bed that afternoon only to answer calls of nature that involved the bathroom, although we answered an even stronger call of nature involving bodies and bed, and more than once. We also talked, a great deal. When the phone rang, I looked at my watch. It was seven-thirty PM.

"Oh, 'allo! Yes, much better," she said in French. "Really. Yes, he is; I think we have talked enough to have written two books about the Crusades, by now. No, I—oh my, so late! Well, perhaps I should just remain where I am—perhaps if I am lucky he will join me for dinner here." As she spoke, she was idly fondling my wilted wang with her free hand. It began to consider unwilting. "Yes. But yes! Fine then, Papa, good night then, and try not to get yourself raped by those teachers!"

She hung up, smiling, and flung both arms around me.

A few minutes later, she advised that it was her father, which I had deduced, and that he had assured her he would not be stopping by her cabin this evening.

"He knows," I said.

She nodded, smiling, a mystical woman's smile. "He knows, but yes. And he is delighted. Oh, Lance!" Then she wept awhile. We got that straightened out, and she called to order dinner for two, there in the cabin. And we got up and dressed to greet the steward and the food with dutiful decorum. And we ate. And talked. And drank, carefully. We made out like crazy, too, eventually getting out of our clothes, and then we piled right back into her bed again.

In her cabin and mine Suzanne and I talked and fondled and held and kissed and made love daily and nightly for the rest of the voyage. It was all wonderful, tingle or not—and no, it wasn't there. But it didn't matter. Sure, we both fell in love. Sure, we talked about it. Sure, we both cried a bit.

And we parted at the top of the gangplank. I read about her wedding, just under two weeks later. Sure, I cried a bit.

CHAPTER SIXTEEN

But once I was off the ship and had my luggage stored in a nice big taxicab, one of those jump-seat affairs that make you wonder if the driver isn't a Don Juan who sometimes pops into the back seat, I didn't have time to mope and feel sorry for myself and try to control my treacherous lachrymal glands. Because I had sudden company. The veiled woman from the ship. She slipped slitherily in beside me. With a gun. It was aimed at me.

"Tell him to drive," she muttered.

Her handbag concealed the little pistol from the driver's inquiring gaze. Sure, he was looking, but he wasn't shook; hell, he was a New York cab-driver.

I told him to drive.

"Now give me that brooch, Lance darling!"

"God damn it, Giulia, I DON'T HAVE THE DAMNED THING!"

"Yes you do, lover," she smirked, lifting her veil with one hand and keeping that gun on me, clutched cleverly close to her hip, with the other. "It's in the lining of your middle-sized suitcase."

I stared at her. "You're really fulla shit, you know that? Now for pete's sake stow away that gun and . . ."

Her eyes narrowed, looking nasty. "Stop that. The brooch is there because I put it there. How nice that Customs didn't check you very carefully at all, you with your sweet ingenuous face and your no-purchases! You have brought it in for me, mother's brooch and all the money it will bring—my ticket to *Hollywood!*"

"Hollywood?"

She lifted her head haughtily, pointing her pretty chin at me. "Hollywood," she repeated. "Where else should a beautiful Italian girl with a beautiful figure go?"

"Jesus," I muttered, then, "How about straight to hell?"

I saw her knuckles whiten a little around the gun. "Tell him to stop now, Lance. I want the brooch, and then you've seen the last of me—in person. Next time you see me, it will be on the big screen!"

"Julie. . . ."

"STOP THE CAB!" she snapped.

We slowed as the driver took his foot off the accelerator, tilting his head to see my face in his mirror. He wasn't braking.

"We don't want to stop *here,* Julie," I tried to tell her, this is . . ."

Tell him!" Suddenly she looked really dangerous. Suddenly I took her seriously. She was nuts. Cracked wide open. Gun in hand. Just a li'l eye-talian girl, straight out of a convent, following the siren call to the land of Opportunity. Another titsy and pretty Italiana ready to go the Sophia Loren route out Los Angeles way.

"Stop here, driver," I said.

"Uh, Mister.. . ."

"Yeah, I know, but the lady's adamant, and thanks for not calling me Mac. Just pull over there in that big empty spot by the curb, OK? Just for a couple of minutes."

So he did, and Julie and I got out, and he came back to open the trunk for us. Out came the suitcase in question. After opening it, I stepped back. Very swiftly, she reached in, slipped her hand in just *there,* and came up with a handsome piece of jewelry. She'd conned me all the way. All the way. No boyfriend, unless it was some poor joker she'd used. Presumably the theft of my overnight case had been pure coincidence. As to the search of my room—I suppose that's when she put the brooch into my suitcase. But then why had she turned up, later? I don't know. Maybe she thought I'd seen her. Maybe she had to double check, to make sure I hadn't found it. Maybe she hadn't got it well concealed and had been scared, when she'd broken in that afternoon and ransacked the place. I *don't know*. I really don't care, either. She had certainly uptighted me more than once, and she had certainly used me.

All in all, I guess it wasn't much of a success as a trip. I sure didn't get relaxed much. And the final business with Suzanne . . . and now this. The driver and I standing there gazing at the scintillant piece of jeweler's art she triumphantly drew out of my luggage. Both of us stared.

She gave me a bright smile. *"Thank* you, darling Lance, for bringing this into the country for me? Now—*ciao!"*

I glanced around. "Giulia—you don't want to be alone in this neighborhood, with that . . ."

"Get into the cab." She waved her stole-wrapped pistol.

The driver slammed the trunk lid and walked around the cab. "Mister, I'm gonna take her advice. She's nutty enough to want to be here, so OK. I don't know what I'm into, but I don't dig it worth shit. You comin'?"

"Julie . . ."

"Get lost, Lance!" Viciously.

I got into the cab. Closed the door. We drove away. I looked out the back window—just in time to see the dude come running out of the tenement on the west side of the street, snatch the brooch out of Giulia's hand on the run, and race into the alley on the east side. I knew she was shrieking by the twisting of her face and the gaping of her mouth. She fired after the running thief, six times. And missed all six times. He vanished. Just as she started to glance after us, we turned a corner. I'd *tried* to warn her about that neighborhood!

"You see that, Mister? What the hell've you got me into?"

"A woman I balled in Italy. She wants to be in pictures, you know? So she stole her own mother's brooch and hid it in my luggage. I didn't know a damned thing about it; you saw that. Then she piled in, just as you and I were driving off, and showed me the gun. You know the rest. I haven't got you into anything. You're not into anything, either, not as long as you and I are both smart enough to just shut up, right?"

"Amen," he said. "Dumb dago bitch."

My driver was a Puerto Rican.

"Bye, Giulia," I murmured, as we drove away and I had a mental vision of her standing there forlornly. A stranger in a strange land. Sans Mamma's brooch, which had cost both her and me so much trouble and anguish. *Bye, Giulia—and after all that trouble, too! Poor baby.*

So I went home, untingled.

Home wasn't just Dad and Martha, now, but Mindy as well, along with her daughter Janey—who still had all the instincts of a vamp. Dad looked great, vigorous and happy. Mindy looked as good as always. Janey looked fine, too, very female, and the kiss the little minx laid on me was a lot more serious and sexy than her mother's. After all; Mindy was now my stepmother. No more soul-kisses.

They wanted me to regale them with accounts of my adventures, of course, and I wanted filling in from them. We managed to work an exchange, during which I learned that Carla-Sable was engaged.

I blinked. "You mean—like—to be married?"

Janey giggled. Smiling, Dad and Mindy nodded. "Like, to be married," Mindy said. "To the guitar player in some New York City punk-rock band. She . . ."

"A *what?*"

"A really super-looking hunk who always wears a leather jacket from straight out of the Fifties . . . like James Dean and Brando and . . . wow!" Janey declaimed avidly.

"A real weird idiot who walks around on stage with a safety pin punched through his cheek who burps like a slob and thinks that's called singing," Dad translated, and I assumed the real description of the dude in question lay somewhere in the approximate center of the generation gap.

Mindy sighed. "Well, he doesn't *seem* much of a catch, but then what does that mean? I have an idea it's Sable's reaction against her mother—who tried to marry her off to some impecunious Italian noble while they were over there."

"Jesus," I said with fervor, and we sort of slid into a conversation about the di Stresas.

That eventually led to the Fanfanis, but I not only didn't talk about my liaison with Giulia or subsequent events with her and stemming from her, I didn't mention the family idea of "hospitality," either. *Later,* I thought. After all, there sat Janey, rapt and excited, coiled like a spring in the gold brocade chair with her chin in her hand and her elbow on her doubled knees, which were pointed at me. So was her face; she stared at me most of that long talky evening. No, I told myself, and reiterated. *The fruits is not yet ripe, despise the fact that she is a most inspiring example of femininity.* She further gave no inclination of an inclination to part our company, even when the day ended and the morning began. Nor did her mother or stepfather mention beddy-bye to her. She stayed right there with us, until nearly two-thirty AM, which was when I allowed as how I'd be moseying along, bedward.

"I'll come along," Janey said, uncoiling and stretching in a way that afforded a spectacular view of her thigh-tops and the way her bra-less breasts resisted the efforts of her clinging shirt to quell their youthful musculature and irrepressible burgeoning brazenness.

"Hardly," I said, with a small but nervous chuckle.

"Oh don't be so libidinously oriented," Janey said scornfully. "I merely meant that I, too, am tired—*not* that I'd come along with *you.*"

I shot Dad a look. He rolled his eyes helplessly. And when I shifted my gaze to Mindy, she merely flashed me an imperturbably indifferent smile. I moved rather swiftly, in order to get upstairs and into bed. Alone. I had a fleeting thought about locking my door, but knew that was ridiculous. Maybe I was a little disappointed at being right, when I awoke next morning. But then I began to think about Suzanne, and that blew away any other thoughts.

I spent the next four days doing labor. I mean physical labor, in one of Dad's warehouses. That helped get my mind off things, things being Suzanne—and, dammit, Janey—and it certainly contributed to my ability to sleep.

On the fifth day after my return, Dad and Mindy mentioned at dinner that Helena was coming to stay with us awhile.

"Helena? You mean—*that* Helena? *Cousin* Helena?"

"Of course, that Helena," Dad said, looking at me as though I'd suddenly gone balmy.

"But—look, it hasn't been—*any time* since you told me she was married!"

He sighed, and decanted a goodly quantity of il Magnifico ruffino into both his glass and mine, which gesture I accepted with both gratitude and renewed thirst for anything alcoholic.

"Well, she isn't now, son. She was in Reno less than a month after the wedding. Since then she's been sort of, ah, wandering." He rolled his eyes in Mindy's direction, but she showed neither approbation nor disapproval of the term. He looked back my way. "She spent the better part of a month in Southern California; understand she explored—ahh, other lifestyles."

Mindy chuckled. "Mabel was frantic that she'd vanish into some Guyana—like cult."

"Aunt Mabel?"

"No, silly, Helena." And Mindy giggling, reached for the wine bottle.

"She didn't," Dad said. "Now she—Helena, Lance, not Mabel—has been home only a little

224

over a week, and she's on tranquilizers already."

"Which?"

Dad heaved a great sigh, but answered with equanimity. "I don't know, son—is the brand of the stuff important?"

"No-no, I meant which of them is on tranquilizers. Look, this is all a bit of a surprise—I mean the last I heard she was getting married, and then you tell me she's coming here for a visit, and now—this other stuff. Helena in some cult?" I shook my head, and hoisted my wine glass, and tried to inhale the bottom out of it.

"It's Helena who's on the tranks," Janey supplied.

I glanced her way to give her a smallish look of appreciation for information, and received in return a positively stupefying smile. Beautiful. Rather like Mindy, and suddenly my flabbergasted mind was seized with a wild idea; a perfectly intemperate idea—a marvelous one. Hope dawned over me like a lightbulb above my head. But then I had to drag my attention back to what Dad was saying, still about Cousin Helena—about whom who gave a dollop of dung?

"Yes, it's Helena who's on the medication, son. Because of Mabel, who is constantly, ah . . ."

"—on her ass about it," Janey calmly supplied.

"Cousin Helena," I suggested satirically, "doesn't have enough ass for anyone to get on!"

Mindy and Janey broke up; Dad affected to look mildly shocked and accusative. I then affected to look apologetic, probably succeeding only in achieving an expression of simpering sanctimoni-

225

ousness; I didn't *feel* apologetic. I *did* feel Janey's leg; I had slipped my foot out of my house-slipper and was caressing her calf with my toes. She pressed it closer, after an initial twitch and astonished look. Smiled like Mindy, did she? Mindy's daughter, eh?

"So we thought we'd just let her stay with us awhile, Lance," Dad was continuing.

"Helena," Mindy put in, but he gave no indication of having heard her. He went on with his unfinished sentence:

"—while she looks around Manhattan. She needs to find something that interests her and get into it."

"More likely," Mindy calmly informed him, "something interesting that will get into her!"

"Well don't look at me!" I cried with heavy emphasis, and Martha stuck her head and questioning eyebrows out of the kitchen. "Brandy," I suggested. The il Magnifico had become a deceased warrior. And my head was still in turmoil. Not just about the Helena news, either.

"Maybe you can help her, Lance," Dad said.

Now that *was* what I needed, all right. Something interesting to get into. But I wasn't interested in getting into the uninteresting Helena Holliman. Or whatever her last name was now.

"Sure," I said. "I've got all kinds of connections. Ah, thank you, Martha—anyone else?"

"Snifters all around," Dad said.

"Don't forget, that movie starts at eight," Mindy said.

Dad checked his watch. "Snifters all around,

226

Martha. What connections, Lance?"

"Umm. I wonder if, perhaps, Cousin Helena can find her way around New York City—and play guitar in a punk-rock band!"

Dad made an exasperated face; Mindy rolled her eyes; Janey giggled. "Or maybe she could be the lead singer. She might even be the next Blondie!"

Janey got up and did a far-from-bad imitation of the cute, blonde punk-rocker, and we all complimented her . . . except for Dad.

"Have you ever heard Sable's beau play?" Janey inquired of me.

"No, can't say as I have. I'm not too into punk-rock music . . . except for the Rolling Stones . . . the *original* punk-rock band. Have you ever heard Helena sing?" I responded.

Things had gotten to be fun And Dad and Min—Mon were going to a movie. Perfect!

None of us had ever heard Helena sing *or* play, as it turned out, and none of us was particularly anxious for either experience. We talked about it a little, with me getting a cramp, messing around with Janey's leg with my foot. Then Mindy and Dad had to go and get ready for the movie.

"It's that film with Kate Hepburn and Hank and Jane Fonda," Mindy said. " 'On Golden Pond.' We didn't get a chance to see it before Kate and Hank took the Academy Awards for their performances. Now everyone and his uncle will be standing in the lines to see it. Want to come along?"

"I think I'll take a raincheck; I'm a bit bushed,"

I said.

"I'd only go along if *Peter* Fonda was in it. I really love him."

We all smiled, and the movie-goers were getting ready to leave.

Janey and I hung together, helping Martha clear off the table and then suggesting, with Janey following my lead, that we wash up while Martha went to the movie, too.

"Perhaps I shouldn't," Martha sniffed.

"Oh Martha, for pete's sake," I expostulated, squeezing her shoulder. "Live a little."

"Henry Fonda is in it," Janey sagaciously said, for she knew that Martha was and had long been a fan of his acting.

"We'll be back about ten-thirty," Dad said, staring at me with a towel in one hand and a saucer in the other as if he wanted to record the astonishing and doubtless disedifying sight forever on his memory spools.

"No we won't," Mindy said, clutching his arm firmly. "We're going to take Martha out for a drink afterward, and it'll be at least midnight!"

"Well, try to behave," I bade them all, and found I couldn't go so far as to ask Martha if she'd taken her birth-control pill. "Keep an eye on Dad, Mindy. I've seen him eyeing Martha all week."

Martha giggled, Dad looked mildly shocked, and Mindy laughed. And they departed.

"How come you don't have a date on a Saturday night, lady?" I asked.

Janey shrugged, up to her elbows in suds; she'd

squirted enough liquid dishwasher in the sink to clean up after a banquet. "Beats me—why don't *you?*"

"Beats me, been working too hard. Want to be my date?"

"Sure, us kitchen help oughtta stick together. How about if you tell me the *real* story about your trip?"

"What real story?" I set aside another cup and picked up a wet one.

"You know. You can't kid me, Romeo. You must've made out in five different languages!"

I counted up. Did Martinique French count as different from French-French? Did Britishcount as foreigh language from our language, what ever it is? Hell, for that matter, did Texican count as English?

"Nine, morelike," I said in a deliberately casual voice. "If you count dialects."

"NINE!" she turned huge eyes on me, her eyebrows seeking her hairline. "Now you're putting me on."

"Well, maybe it was eight."

"I don't believe you."

I shrugged. "It was your idea, remember. Just trying to make you happy."

She regarded me for a moment, thoughtfully, her hands buried in the dishwasher. (We had a dishwasher installed once. Martha didn't like it. So she destroyed it. With a frightful noise. Something in the engine. And we're missing a fork to the best set.)

"Name them," Janey said challengingly, cocking

229

her head and regarding me with cool eyes, her eyebrows arrnaged in postures of disbelief. "Just name then then, Don Juan."

"Don Giovanni," I said, thinking of the opera and that clown's long catalog of the lover's conquests. "And in Hispania-a-a-a . . ." I smiled at the thought. Then I said, "Italian. Ummm—four."

"Four what?" All dishwashing activity had ceased. The front of her sleeveless print blouse was rising and falling faster and faster.

"Four women. Then . . ."

"Name them."

"The women?"

She nodded, eyes closed schoolmarmishly.

"Oh come *on,* Janey. You don't really . . ."

"You can't. You're putting me on. You *couldn't* have. Not even you." Then she looked as if she wanted to bite her tongue. She'd slipped.

"Don't worry about it, Janey," I said, "I already know."

"Already know what?"

"Already know that you're warm for my form."

"What?"

"Hot to trot. Longin's for a dongin'."

"Ugh! That's—obscene!"

"Ready for beddy?"

"You—you are disgusting!"

"Leave, then. I'll finish washing up."

She sighed. "Bastard. Are you really as old as they say you are?"

"Are you really as young as they say you are?"

Again she heaved a sigh. "Oh damn you."

"Can we forget the litany, now?"

230

She had returned her attention, or at least her manual motions, to the dishes. "Litany? What—oh. No. Name those Italian girls."

"Women," I corrected, and then I went on in a matter-of-fact tone, "Rafaela, in Roma. Constanza, in a castle above Rome. Don't look at me that way—you asked. She's a contessa. Or at least her daddy's a count. With a huge old castle and exactly one servant. Very anxious to marry Connie off to money?"

"Connie?"

"You don't think I called her Contessa in bed, do you?"

"You—you are . . ."

"You haven't used 'insufferable' yet," I said helpfully.

"Gee Lance, I'm not sure I even like you anymore."

"Dammit, this whole subject got brought up out of the blue by *you!* I don't want to tell you about all those women and all those languages. What could Elisabetta and Giulia possibly mean to you?

"E-Elisabetta and Julia? Who are they?"

"The other two Italians." I decided against mentioning that they were mother and daughter. Also that one of them had greeted me in my room wearing a nun's habit. After all!

Hunched a little over the sink, she twisted her head to stare at me. "You—you really did. Four women. In Italy." Her smooth forehead was creased in a little frown.

I sighed. "Let's wash dishes and watch TV."

"I don't want to watch TV," she said, passing

over another plate.

"OK, let's talk. Not about my amours."

"I—I think . . . I don't think I want to hear about them. But . . ." At last she exchanged a smile for the frown. "But it is—just fascinating. You know."

"I know, Janey," I said. "That's why Martha went to see Henry Fonda tonight with the folks. She'll love it. Good thing they didn't take her to a sexy movie. Martha would come back saying 'They shouldn't show things like that. People shouldn't even *do* things like that!'"

She chuckled, felt around in the water, and dumped in the silverware. "Well—I guess I do sort of want to hear all that stuff. But I also don't—do not!"

"OK. What about if I *show* you?"

Janey froze. Staring straight ahead, which happened to be into the dishwasher.

"Show—me?"

I put down dish and towel, moved behind her, and slid my hands slowly around her. And up. Until they encountered the nice round pads of her breasts. I moved my hands on up, treating those sweet swells as if they were fragile indeed. She shivered. Silverware rattled. My loins were pressed against her buttocks, which were singularly firm. I was glad that Janey was the legal age; I didn't really feel like going to the slammer for sleeping with my erstwhile mistress's underage daughter. But there was one real complication. That was the possibility that maybe, just maybe, Mindy's *daughter* had inherited whatever it was in Mindy that sent

232

that delicious tingle through me when we made it—
used to make it. I had decided I had to find out,
had to make the attempt. And Janey's behavior in
the past, as well as now that I was home again with
her under the same roof, clearly indicated that she
was indeed warm for my form.

"Oh, ohhh Je-sus," she said, and she shivered.

"Hurry up with those things and let's make it," I
murmured, pushing my lips into her hair and close
to her ear.

"What thi—oh. To *hell* with these things! Oh—
ahhh—oh—damn, oh shi—listen, Lance you
aren't just teasing me?"

"Were you just teasing me when you came on
strong at the wedding, and the same way when I
got home, and flirting like crazy ever since?" I had
my hands pressed over her unbrassiered breasts,
moving each finger, but only a little and without
much pressure.

"Uh—yes . . . Yes and no. . . ."

I gave her breasts a last little squeeze, just a little
one, and stepped back. "Well, get the silver done,
Janey-babe, and let's go turn on the TV."

"TEE-VEE!" She swung her round blue eyes my
way. Her face was flushed. "TELEvision!"

I blinked, as if I couldn't understand her perturbation. She stared. Then she said, in a small voice,
"You *were* teasing."

"I shook my head. "No, I wasn't. But you just
said you were. And I don't take advantage of any
. . ."

Which is how and when I got soapsuds all over
the sides and back of my shirt, because she swung

233

away from the sink and slammed herself against me, gripping me with both hands on my back, ramming her vehemently firm young breasts into me and wiggling her shoulders, rubbing me with her boobs, ramming her mouth up hard against mine and kissing hell out of me. Her lips were well parted, and she moaned and pushed harder against me when my tongue explored the soft inner reaches of her mouth. With one hand I held her waist; with the other I caressed her lower hip and thigh, just where it emerged from her abbreviated skirt.

Somehow or another, without breaking apart, we got out of the kitchen and up the steps and into her bedroom, and then we were on the bed still making out and with her eyes open, all misty, while I kissed her and used my hand all over her breasts, then opened her blouse, slowly and with a pause to slip my fingers exploratorially inside between the loosening of each button. She was writhing, nibbling at my lips, caressing them with her pointed little teasing tongue.

Then I peeled open her blouse, baring a truly lovely pair of firm, barely resilient breasts with large lovely areolas and no nipples at all. But they appeared when I stroked with my fingers, appeared and asserted themselves very definitely; up and out the pretty pink nubbins zoomed, the big areolas shrinking but remaining centered perfectly about their mini-erections.

I spent long minutes kissing and suckling the impatient, thick points. Her hands roamed all over me, fully clothed as I was, and she sighed and moaned in an almost continual hum.

Then she was groaning more loudly; my hand was gliding, gliding, coaxing her skirt up as the fingers moved up, until I could feel the soft bulging shape of her vulva beneath the wispy nylon sheath of her panties. Her hands tangled in my hair, then clenched in little spasms while I pampered her pantied crotch with a delicate massage of all four fingers. She grated out a throaty groan in a sudden fierce ecstasy of aroused sensuality, and rammed her mound up against my hand as if seeking to bruise the tender lips.

"I—you—ahhh," she sighed, unable to get the words out. "Don't—you—gahh!"

"Shh," I told her breast, "enjoy!"

"I want . . ."

"You'll get."

"I want you out of—ahh!—those damned clothes, man, I want your body naked and mine, too, mi—unnnngh!—mine, toooo! Please—Lance—STOP!"

I stopped. She trembled violently. Then we got naked. Without getting up, a lot of scrambling around on the bed and a lot of touching and mutual help that wasn't help at all but that was a lot of fun anyhow.

Then she didn't want anything but me inside her, and that quickly, and she made it unconditionally and consummately clear.

"Stop treating me like some little virgin you're breaking in, man, ram me and cram me!"

I squeezed my eyes closed. That really isn't my sort of bedroom talk. Suddenly I knew, and that was not pleasant knowledge. It wasn't going to be there. It was going to be just a lay, and with a girl I'd have to live with in the same _house_, and I wished I hadn't started it.

But the Marquis de Verchamp had called me a gentleman, and I guess I am. Too much of a gentleman not to screw when screwing is called for. Loudly.

So we screwed.

Her throaty cries certainly did not detract from my delight in pushing up inside that warm and sublimely tight nook that she hunched up to me. I actually shoved in, implanting my cock the rest of the way between firm-pressing inner folds with a vicious thrust that made her cry out—in an agony of pleasure. Her hands and arms clamped me. Her body shivered and stiffened and she came, just like that, marvelously. That inner response of her so-youthful body thrilled me and filled me with a soaring feeling of pride and delight and power.

Propping myself above her on my elbows so that she had the feel and heat and pressure of my body within its weight, I waited, smiling down at her. She was flinging her head back and forth, streaming perspiration. No, sweat. Perspiration is for ladies, and ladies don't fuck, they have intercourse, and I really doubt that they come like cannons, either. Or like oily vises, because that's what I felt all around my trapped prick. Catch me complaining!

Then she was limp for a few seconds, and then she looked up at me with very bright eyes. She flashed her teeth in another of those dazzling smiles of hers.

"Boy do you feel good in me! That's the best

come I've had in—weeks! Ever!" She squeezed me, hands and cunt. "Beautiful! GLOrious! Now, now, you screw me, Lance Holliman, beautiful Lance, and make it good oh good, Lance, because we're like stepbrother and stepsister, and we have to live here, and this is never ever going to happen again!"

"You're right," I told her, thinking *unless I feel that tingle, Janey-girl,* and I started moving.

She did to, and her frenetic motions beneath me built up a swift, almost unbearable tension in my balls that became an inner pressure. I half withdrew and ceased moving. Then I thought, to hell with it, I am good for two, and, pausing only long enough to smile down at her suddenly stricken face and wiggled my hips, I pushed back in, slowly. She breathed out a long sigh of pleasure, the darling labial folds around the mouth of her twat feeding inward as I sank slowly back into her.

She began moving again, squirming with increasing passion, grinding her cunt around and around the big prong splitting open the delicate tissues inside her. Every movement, hers and mine, intensified both my passion and my need, the desire to blow my balls into the tender trap of wet flesh surrounding my cock. I pushed and pulled, probing and probing at that hot drenched gap, until I blew up in a violent orgasm that drenched it still more.

And I kept right on fucking. Minute after minute, with her staring up at me with delightedly surprised eyes. I was no longer hard, only the super lubrication I had added to kept me from flopping out of her. But then it began again, the process of tumescence demanding detumescence.

We rolled. I screwed her facing her, on our sides, or rather we screwed each other that way. And I rolled her onto her back again, driving hard, an inordinately lusty missionary indeed, and surprised her by lifting her left leg, doubling it, letting her feel that changed and thus new probing for a while, then getting her leg across between us, across my chest and belly, until both her legs were on my left and forced high with my scrotum rapping her lovely rearward curves. Eventually we both moved, so that I was spooned up behind her, slapping her butt hard with my hips and loins. Eventually we moved again, with her groaning, flat on her belly, and my kneeling up behind her, crouching, while she panted and thrust herself back, voluptuously wriggling her firm-cheeked butt to caress me with it—and to caress my cock inside the slick sheath beneath those round pads.

I wanted to come with her under me, and I pulled all the way out. She started to cry out in despair, but she had been rolled over and again filled before the lament was finished. Her fingers dug at me as she balled back, her body singing in response to the constant hot skewering. I think she came when I did; at least she said so. By that time we were both hot and sweaty, which for me is a Good. The making of love—screwing—shouldn't be a cool, sweatless activity. Not to me, anyhow.

A long time after that second time I had exploded inside her, she sighed out, "I—I think I—must have been hasty in saying what I said. . . ."

238

"But we're going to stick with it, right, little sister?" I said, and she chuckled at the final words and sighed again:

"Yeah. Yeah, Lance—big brother."

Which was the way it had to be. I'd been kidding myself, and now I was more than glad that, once again, I had not experienced the strange tingling sensation in the lower abdomen that I had experienced with her mother, and sought elsewhere so long, and now was resigned to living without.

CHAPTER SEVENTEEN

Enter Helena, with a large amount of luggage and a lovely tan.

She was—different.

I worked at that, eyeing her; we'd greeted each other pretty coolly. Or rather she had come on that way, and I had responded. What do you say after you say hello?—nothing. I realized that her staying here wasn't going to be too complicated, at that. We were, apparently, nodding acquaintances; I'd say nodding to her and she'd say nodding to me.

But I puzzled over her *difference*. What was it? Different—how?

Hell, older, more womanly looking, with more—confidence? Something like that. Awareness of herself as a woman, maybe; self-awareness that was awareness of Self, rather than merely the self-consciousness that had been there before. I realized that she must have been a virgin.

"I imagine so," Dad said, when I mentioned it to him.

"Well, it's done her a world of good, getting her pipes blown out," I said.

He smiled. That wasn't really his kind of talking, but he's far from a fogey. "I'm sure it does us all a lot of good, son."

I smiled. "I guess she was—anxious to shed it," I mused aloud. *No wonder she went so far as to call up a nasty dirtymouthed arrogant SOB like me!* And then, rejected and really nastily hit, I reflected with a bit of guilt, *and then took off with a—a scumball!* Because she wanted to be a woman, because she was tired of being a virgin, tired of Aunt Mabel, too, I'll bet!

But there was something else different about her, and it actually took pore old dumb Lance a couple of days to realize. AHA! *The bitch had miraculously developed a better bod!*

Let's see, what have I said about her? How did I remember her—a way that she no longer was, a mold she no longer fit?

At the wedding I had noted, on the positive side, that she was pretty, that her rather angular face possessed a perfectly beautiful bone structure. OK; now she was prettier. I had characterized her as being unaware of herself as a woman, unknowledgeable how to decorate herself; as too tall, with not enough meat on her, which I guess is a pretty ugly phrase; old-fashioned male-looking-at-object.

Well, she was still only an inch or so shorter than I, but now she looked as if she weighed in at a bit more than the skimpy hundred pounds I'd gauged her at. Filled out, people call it; Helena *had* filled out. Nicely. Furthermore, she knew now how to drape that filled-out figure. Her clothes no longer looked as if they'd been picked out by Aunt Mabel—blindfolded. And drunk. They looked good. Modern. *She* looked good.

In person she used to come off cucumber-cool, though easily shocked out of that cool. A bit—mousey? In Aunt Mabel's (large) shadow. On the phone, though, Helena had sounded soft and cuddly, a strange paradox. Now she *looked* that way, which isn't easy at five-ten. Her red-brown hair was longer, too, and worn natural, caressing her shoulders softly and framing that fine-boned face.

Filled out?

AHA! *The bitch has taken to wearing* FALSIES!

So, after she'd been there five days, after a businessman's week of that coolness between us, an armed truce, I decided to blow her cool again. What did I do?

I deliberately walked into the bathroom where she was taking a bath.

And stared. With her staring back, though with her face arranged in an entirely different expression from mine. She brought her legs together, mostly concealing the nice patch of fur that was paler, more red and less brown than the hair on her head. Too, after the first few shocked seconds, she crossed her arms over her chest. Which bulged over those tanned arms.

"My—my God!"

"I think," she said, with amazing sang-froid, "that that's *my* line, Cousin Lancelot."

"You—you DO have ti—breasts! You DON'T wear falsies!"

I saw her eyes flash, but she impressed me again; obviously her determination to maintain her equanimity prevailed. "No," she levelly replied. "I do not. Once I began to take the pill, and once I, ah, discovered what this body was for, things began to happen to it. And to my head. My getting married was stupid, and I admit it. But it did me a lot of good."

What do you say to a naked lady in a tub after an admission like that? Since when did honesty replace games-playing? I stood there, frozen, staring. She didn't look like Ingrid Pitt, but she sure did look like a woman, even though she was pretty meatless elsewhere. Or I should say slim, slender, svelte; something nicer than "meatless," right?

"Well?" Sitting there naked in the tub, she asked in a collected voice, "Do I look like a good lay?"

Throwing my own words to her mother back at me! And I was all ready to give her a truthful answer, too—when the imp of perversity somehow seized control of my tongue, the little bastard.

"Frankly," I said, "no."

"You BAStard! Get OUTTA here!" And she scooped up a slippery bar of soap and, with astonishing aim, bounced the damned thing off my head.

I retreated. I went to my room. Undressed, put on a robe, tried to read. But my mood wasn't his, and my thoughts just wouldn't cooperate, so I laid Jerzy Kosinski aside and scoured around for something else. Well, there was the cloth edition of John Updike's 'Rabbit Redux,' which I'd bought about a dozen years ago, but never got the chance to read to completion. Unfortunately, it was sex . . . just like Kosinski's stuff. Now I enjoy reading sexy books, but—not at present. I had gone a week or so in monkish celibacy, and had just left a nekkid woman in the tub.

I kept thinking back to the loveliness I'd seen; the womanliness. And the unallayed demands of my body were intrusive not only on reading, but on keeping my thoughts on the book—and on relaxation. I was aware of a large supply of muscles that refused to relax. The worst was the one in my groin.

Finally I discarded that book, too, and went silently downstairs to return with a snifter containing several ounces of nice warm brandy. On the way, I picked up one of Dad's books—Marine law. Back in my room, aware that the bathroom door was open and the room thus unoccupied and that there was a line of light beneath Helena's door, I reposed myself with brandy and dull book. Feet up on the bed. I sipped and inhaled and read.

Or tried to. Not even the supreme dullness of that stupid book, though, commingled with the brandied air with which I was becoming emfumed, succeeded in moving me any nearer to the threshold of sleep.

Couldn't get sex out of my mind. Couldn't get Helena out of my mind. At least I did something quite uncharacteristic; I flung the book across the bed so that it bounced off the wall on the other side, and I put down the brandy, unfinished.

To hell with it! Hell! What the hell, I'll do it! I'll go rape hell out of Helena!

So I did.

The only trouble was, she was sitting up in bed, knees up, reading a book. And she was quite beautifully bereft of clothing.

"Good lord," she said without a great deal of indication of shock or fear, "you again? Is this your thing, Lance, hanging out in and out of rooms where I am *en deshabille?*— and without so much as a tiny little knock?"

I closed the door behind me and advanced upon bed and Helena.

"I came to—to apologize," I said.

A look of some surprise settled on her face, then was replaced by one of nascent warmth. She looked up at me; I now stood over her bed. Her lower body, knees still up, was covered with the topsheet. She had pulled her book back to her, so that it and her arms sort of covered her breasts. The book was without its dust jacket, and it was black. I recognized it at once, and wondered if it was her first time to read *Story of O.*

"Really?" she asked.

I took a deep breath. Heart pounding like a kid about to put the grabs on a penny on the sidewalk. Then I said, "No, actually I came to rape you," and I went after her throat with one hand while using the other to push her knees down and thus get her body into the most rapable posture.

Naturally enough, she bonked me with the book. And again. I winced, grunted, and saw some bright lights. Then I dragged the damned thing out of her hands, whereupon it became the second book to be hurled across a room by me in five or six minutes.

Flopping onto the bed with her, I began a wrestling match in which she stoutly essayed to keep the topsheet over her most intimate parts while I strove just as doggedly to tug it downward and expose more than the few darling red curls poking out above it. With my other hand I was pressing her down, hand on her chest just above the eminent extrusions of her newborn breasts—while she pulled my hair—or rather tangled her fingers in it and pushed.

That pain I endured, forcing my head down and down, until my lips came into conjunction, with, first, one of those titillatingly twinned tits, and then with the nice little pink mushroom that tipped it so fetchingly. She gasp-groaned. Her arm trembled and some of the pressure at my hair—which was bringing tears to my eyes from the pressure on my lachrymal glands—eased up. Applying considerable suction, I sucked the saucy little nubbin into my mouth and stretched the seemingly willing flesh. I tugged hard at it with a deep-cheeked suction.

"Uh," she commented, "ah—annngh—L—La—Lanssssse. . . ."

I let go the sheet and plunged my hand beneath

it. My fingers came instantly into contact with baby-soft hair, then brushed the lobes that pretended to guard the damp little slit nestled there. Again she groaned. Her thighs clamped my hand, hard, but I felt the shiver and knew it was a helplessly erotic tremor of anticipation dancing through her loins. My fingertips found the proper spot at the very top of that softly-slit delicacy, and began rubbing.

Gasping, she let her legs drift wide to accept any sort of caress I cared to bestow on that semi-sheathed button or pure sensation. It wriggled partway up out of its sheath.

I made a growling sound around her nipple, which I was now lapping like a cat at a bowl of milk. "Arrhh—easy victim!"

"Wh—when r-rape is in-inevi-ah-table," Helena sighed, sinking back, "relax-x-x—and enjoyyyyy it. . . ."

I licked, sucked, and twiddled. She gasped again, and her thighs parted more, and then her firm little labia dropped open to invite invasion. I invaded, using a finger, which made her squeak and shiver. The breasts against my face had swelled up into balloon-tautness, and their nipples were like bullets. Pressing well up inside her, I then began to withdraw my finger—and felt her strong-gripping labia lock stubbornly on it. When I pulled out, the abandoned lips snapped vibrantly shut as if seeking to snatch at the retreating finger.

So much was I enjoying myself, and so much was she enjoying what I was doing, that I lost sight of my original goal of rape.

I knew she was fresh from a bath, and after many minutes of mouth-on-breast and hand-on-crotch, I backed along her body. For a moment I gazed down at her pretty vulva, then I closed the distance between my lips and the softer pink ones of her cunt. Kneeling between long, satin-soft thighs, I teased with my tongue at one full vaginal lip until she moaned, jerked, and clutched at me in unabashed delight. Her legs snapped in, clamping my head in welcome grip of warm flesh, then splayed wide in total abandon to sensation as I sucked strongly at her little love-button.

I kept my mouth there, one hand outstretched to tickle her nipples, until my tongue was sore. But I couldn't bring her off. She was sighing, moaning, thrashing around, almost sobbing. It was good, I knew that. But I couldn't be sure whether the almost tearful sounds were of joy or frustration. Was her ultimate joy locked up inside her in that ugly, ugly word—frigidity?

I didn't know, but my tongue was sore and I wanted her very much, and when I forsook her core with my mouth and moved swiftly up to penetrate it with my meat, she was as joyous as I at the swift, easy entry.

To hell with rape, I thought, and settled into a long, slow easy balling that we both loved. Time after time I raised myself on my palms and kept us joined only at our sexual centers, our loins forming a fulcrum, and then when my arms began to quiver with strain I lowered myself onto her again. With a woman of her height it was easy to keep myself inside her and get my mouth on her tits at the same time. I did that. Her hands rubbed my ass, just one more plus.

It was all so good, so gloriously intensely extraordinarily good that it wasn't until after I had erupted and was lying gasping in her arms that I realized.

It was there! I had felt that fantastic tingle for many minutes, and taken if for granted, because everything else was so good. The *tingle!*

"My God," I gasped. "So—so *good,* Helena!" I was so happy that I was shivering. She held me in motherly arms, pressing her mouth into my hair and making little crooning sounds.

"Oh, oh yes, darling!"

Then we moved and settled into a long session of kissing and stroking, fondling, palpating. I felt it when it happened; my newly thickened organ rising rigidly from my groin and pulsing intimately against her little belly. Her hand slipped down between us.

"Ummm," she breathed into my mouth, "see what I've found!"

"See what you *did,*" I corrected.

"*Feel* what I did," she re-corrected.

"*You* feel it."

She did. Her forefinger and thumb tightened around that throbbing stalk, just behind the knobby head, and slowly, firmly, she pulled it forward.

I didn't wait for her to tuck me into the warm, tight-lipped pinkness of her again. "This time," I said, moving swiftly and roughly, "it's what I promised—RAPE!"

"Eek," she said, totally without enthusiasm or volume. But then she made a semi-pained grunting sound, for I lurched into her and touched bottom on the instant.

My hands clamped onto her breasts as if I hated them. My thumbs came down onto the tips of the nipples, and pushed, and pushed, until the pink extrusions vanished into the white flesh and I could feel her ribs far beneath. Through the resilient pads of her boobs, I rolled her nipples over her ribs. And ground forcefully into her. Again and again I plunged into the grasping channel between her hungry thighs, and again and again I plunged back with berserker force. Our bodies slapped together with noisy impacts. Both of us began to be slippery wet. Even the air of her bedroom became redolent with the wonderful aroma of sex. And I drove on, and drove, and drove. . . .

Suddenly her eyes flared wide. She went board-stiff beneath my pounding driving body. Everyone in the house must have heard the shrill cry that announced her arrival at the peak. The silken walls of her vaginal depths spasmed and convulsed around me as she sighed and jerked her way to the ultimate fulfillment. I paused, glorying in her climax, in my success in bringing it on, and then I began pounding again, and soon joined her in toppling over the cliff of orgasm mountain.

We lay exhausted for a long long while.

Then, soft-voicedly: "L-Lance—darling— what—what happened? That was—I've never— my God, I really *came!*"

I propped up onto one elbow to gaze into her

face. My hand was drawn automatically to one now-soft breast, and I caressed it gently.

"You're serious, Helena? You've never. . ."

She was shaking her head. Tears glistened on her cheeks. At last she said, trying to smile, "You—you *bastard,* you nasty arrogant bastard—you made me come! Oh Lance I love you!" And she was all over me, her body and arms and mouth unable to get enough of me. We occupied ourselves in that kind of wonderful activity for a while, a long while. Then she rolled away and lay grinning at me.

"Wow," she said dreamily, "I never felt anything even approaching this with the greasy super-macho clown I married! You, Lance, *are* a good lay!"

I soared. She was saying that to me—this woman who had at last made me feel that long-sought tingle again! Talk about a mutual admiration society!

I leaned over her; she was gazing mistily at the wall. "Helena."

She looked up, sighed, smiled, and put both hands on me again. "Hmmm?"

"Helena, you are a good lay!"

We began laughing, holding each other as we laughed, and eventually we made it again, me feeling heroic, and she screamed again when she came, and thank God nobody came a-running!

I never did get back to my room. I didn't want to leave her. Maybe I was almost afraid to. And she didn't want me to leave her. Similar reasons. We just didn't want to let each other go.

So we didn't. And haven't.

We relented, finally and even invited Aunt Mable to the wedding. She acted shocked when I told her that Helena was a damned good lay. But the old broad came to the wedding, anyhow.